THE DANGEROUS
RESCUE

JEDI APPRENTICE

JEDI APPRENTICE

The Dangerous Rescue

Jude Watson

SCHOLASTIC INC.

New York Toronto London Auckland Sydney
Mexico City New Delhi Hong Kong

Scholastic Children's Books
Commonwealth House, 1-19 New Cxford Street, London WC1A 1NU
a division of Scholastic Ltd
London — New York — Toronto — Sydney — Auckland
Mexico City — New Delhi — Hong Kong

Published in the UK by Scholastic Ltd, 2001
Published in the USA by Scholastic Inc., 2000

ISBN 0 439 99324 5

1 3 5 7 9 10 8 6 4 2

Printed in the USA

THE DANGEROUS RESCUE

CHAPTER 1

Obi-Wan Kenobi heard the door slide shut behind him. The locking system clicked and whirred.

He stopped short as a wave of helplessness overwhelmed him.

"No," he said.

His companion, Astri Oddo, turned. "What is it?"

Obi-Wan faced the closed door with despair. "I can't leave him."

"But he ordered you to go."

Placing his hands against the door, Obi-Wan shook his head. "I can't."

Astri waited a moment. She did not move, but he felt her impatience. Her newly shaved head gleamed in the faint gray light. A heavy mist fell like rain and gathered in droplets on their skin.

"Obi-Wan, we don't have time," she said. "I have to get to the Temple."

Obi-Wan nodded, but still he could not move. Astri's father, Didi Oddo, was dying at the Jedi Temple. Astri carried the antitoxin that would save him. Astri had been a chef at her father's café, and she had bravely joined Obi-Wan in his bold plan to break into Jenna Zan Arbor's secret lab.

They had succeeded in only part of their mission. They had retrieved the needed antitoxin. But Obi-Wan's Master, Qui-Gon Jinn, was still inside.

Obi-Wan spun around and gazed quickly down the dark street, searching every shadow. "Where are Cholly, Weez, and Tup? They can arrange transport for you."

"They're not here," Astri said, anger tightening her voice as she scanned the street. "I knew we couldn't trust them."

Obi-Wan dismissed the thought of the three scoundrels. They had agreed to watch for Ona Nobis, the bounty hunter who Astri had impersonated to get inside. They were supposed to warn Obi-Wan and Astri if she arrived, but they had not. As a result, Jenna Zan Arbor had known that intruders were inside, and Qui-Gon had been trapped. Obviously, Cholly, Weez, and Tup had fled.

But they weren't important to Obi-Wan now. Getting Astri back to the Temple was. As was getting himself back into the secret lab so that he could fight side by side with his Master.

"Let me contact Tahl," he said. Astri handed him her comlink. He had already given his own to Qui-Gon, along with his lightsaber.

Jedi Knight Tahl's crisp voice came through a moment later. "I'm here," she said tersely.

Quickly, Obi-Wan outlined the situation. "Jenna Zan Arbor is holding another prisoner who she claims Qui-Gon doesn't know, but who is close to him. What do you think that means?"

"I have an idea," Tahl said. "Go on."

"Poison will be released in the prisoner's bloodstream if Qui-Gon leaves the building. He ordered me to leave the lab and conduct Astri back to the Temple. He said that safe passage for the antitoxin was the most important thing. I . . . felt I had to go, Tahl."

"Of course you did," Tahl said crisply. "Qui-Gon was right to order you. But I don't want you to leave Simpla-12."

Obi-Wan felt relief flood through him. He was only a Padawan Learner. He would need the permission of a Jedi Master in order to disobey Qui-Gon, even if his Master was currently a captive.

"What about Didi?" Astri asked urgently.

"Don't worry, Astri. Jedi Master Adi Gallia and her Padawan, Siri, are due to arrive on Simpla-12 at any moment. You should see their ship in a few seconds. The pilot can bring you back to the Temple with the antitoxin. Obi-Wan, you will work with Adi Gallia and Siri to rescue Qui-Gon. We'll start with a small team, but we're sending more Jedi to Simpla-12 in case you need them."

Obi-Wan saw a glint of silver in the leaden sky. "I see their ship. I'll get back to you."

He ended the communication and watched as the small, sleek transport landed in a dirt field nearby. He had worked with Adi and Siri before. Adi was a brilliant and resourceful Jedi with a gift for intuition. Siri was a tough fighter and faced danger without ruffling a hair. The relations between the two Padawans could be bumpy, but he could not ask for a better team to rescue Qui-Gon.

He saw Adi's familiar regal figure stride down the landing ramp. The smaller, blond Siri followed. Adi's sharp gaze scanned the surrounding area, missing nothing. Then she hurried toward Obi-Wan and Astri.

She nodded at Obi-Wan and turned her gaze to Astri. "The transport is waiting. May the Force be with you."

Even at a moment of great urgency, Astri thought of others. She put her hand on Obi-Wan's arm. "I know Qui-Gon will be safe."

"And I know Didi will be well," Obi-Wan told her.

They had been through much together. Astri had no Jedi training, no Force-sensitivity, and could barely manage to hit a target with blaster fire. Yet Obi-Wan had come to admire her many skills. Her fear was obvious but she never failed to charge ahead.

Now she fumbled as she withdrew the vibroblade from her belt. "Here. You might need this."

He took it from her. "Thanks. I'll see you back at the Temple."

Biting her lip, Astri nodded. Then she rushed off, wobbling a bit in the thigh-high boots she had donned to impersonate Ona Nobis.

Siri's hand rested lightly on her lightsaber hilt. Her bright blond hair was combed straight back and tucked behind her ears. Her no-nonsense appearance matched the way she attacked a problem. She did not waste time.

"Tahl contacted us a moment ago," she told Obi-Wan. "Zan Arbor has blocked out all communications from the lab, but Qui-Gon managed to get a last message through to the Temple. Zan Arbor has locked herself in with the other prisoner. If Qui-Gon attempts to come through the door, she will kill the captive. He is searching for another way inside that room."

"Did he see the other prisoner?" Obi-Wan asked.

Siri shook her head.

"We think we know who he is," Adi said. "He is a Jedi Master."

Obi-Wan was startled. "She was able to hold *two* Jedi Masters hostage?" How could such a thing happen?

"Noor R'aya is an elder Jedi," Adi explained. "He does not live at the Temple. He no longer goes on missions, but he chose to live out his remaining days in seclusion and meditation on his home planet. He disappeared several weeks ago, and we've been searching for him."

"We traced his disappearance to the bounty hunter, Ona Nobis," Siri explained. "As soon as we told Tahl this, she told us about Jenna Zan Arbor's involvement. Noor R'aya must be the other being Qui-Gon sensed at the lab."

"Our first problem is getting in," Obi-Wan said. "There are no windows and only one door. Other Jedi teams are on their way, but the more we delay, the more we risk Qui-Gon's and Noor R'aya's lives. And Simpla-12 has no security police. It's just us."

"It's not a problem," Adi said serenely. "We have a way in."

"We've learned through our contacts that someone is looking for a large shipment of black market assassin droids for protection on Simpla-12," Adi said. "We know this person is Jenna Zan Arbor. We've tracked down the droid dealers. Now we just need to get the dealers to agree to smuggle us inside along with the shipment."

"When is the transfer supposed to happen?" Obi-Wan asked anxiously.

"As soon as possible," Adi replied. "The droid sellers got the definite impression that Zan Arbor is planning to leave the planet. She could have lied, but I'm guessing her departure plans are behind the urgency of the request. She needs protection in order to leave and she needs protection wherever she goes. She knows the Jedi are on her trail."

"If she's planning to leave, we can't wait for reinforcements," Obi-Wan observed.

Adi nodded grimly. "I agree. Let's head for the warehouse where the droids are being loaded. The sellers are waiting for us."

The warehouse was a dingy metal structure that tilted alarmingly to one side. The foundation was sunk deep into the mud. Simpla-12's constant cloud cover made for frequent rain, and Obi-Wan, Siri, and Adi slogged through ankle-deep mud to reach the entrance.

As Obi-Wan pushed open the door, he heard familiar voices.

"Gibbertz and ham, these droids are old. Couldn't you have found some newer models?"

"Oh, of course, why didn't you say so? Let me reach into my deep pocket full of credits and pay for them."

Obi-Wan groaned aloud. "You don't mean to tell me," he said to Adi and Siri, "that the droid sellers are Cholly, Weez, and Tup?"

"You know them?" Adi asked.

Just then, Cholly caught sight of Obi-Wan. "My friend!" he cried in a warm voice that did not disguise his nervousness.

"Jedi Kenobi!" Weez echoed as Tup slid behind him to hide. "We did not expect you!"

"Why?" Obi-Wan asked, walking toward

them. "Because you thought I was Zan Arbor's prisoner? Because you said you would prevent Ona Nobis from approaching the building, and ran away instead?"

"Well, no," Weez said, shifting his feet nervously. "I wouldn't say that's why."

Tup peeked out from behind him. "We are on your side, Obi-Wan."

"As long as you don't have to risk your own necks," Obi-Wan observed.

"Well, of course," Weez said. "But we are like that with everyone!"

"Wait, let me think. Did we ever say we were brave? I don't think so!" Cholly pointed out.

"And Ona Nobis was a very frightening being," Weez said.

"Woosh," Tup said, blowing out a breath. "You must admit that. But we did follow her!"

"You did?" Obi-Wan asked sharply. "Where did she go?"

"To her own transport," Cholly answered. "She left Simpla-12, we know that."

At least they had given him one piece of information. Ona Nobis was gone for good. She had told Zan Arbor that she would not work for her any longer. She had more profitable clients.

"You can make it up to me now," Obi-Wan said, frowning. "You let the Jedi down once. Do not do it again."

"Never, never, never," Weez said, shaking his head.

"Unless there is terrible danger," Tup added quickly.

"This shouldn't be dangerous for you," Adi said. "All we want you to do is let us hide in your shipment of droids to Zan Arbor. We will find a way to sneak out after you have left."

"Ah," Cholly said. "That would be *after* we get paid, then?"

"Yes," Adi said impatiently. "We just need a way into the building."

Cholly, Weez, and Tup exchanged glances.

"Excuse me so much for asking this," Cholly said. "But what is in it for us?"

"In other words, it sounds risky," Weez explained helpfully. "And there's no reward for our risk."

"Well, we're not going to pay you," Adi said. She fixed her dark, commanding gaze on the three, who squirmed at her scrutiny. "Is that what you are suggesting?"

"Of course not," Tup said stoutly.

"Unless, of course, getting into the lab is very important to you — important enough to pass along a few credits . . ." Cholly's voice trailed off when Adi continued to stare at him. "It was just a thought," he added weakly.

"How about this," Siri suggested in a pleasant tone. "You help us or we'll smash all your droids."

"Siri!" Adi's voice was sharp. "Jedi do not threaten."

Siri's mouth closed, but she continued to stare fiercely at Cholly, Weez, and Tup, her hand on the hilt of her lightsaber.

"I have two reasons you should help us," Obi-Wan said, trying to keep the impatience from his voice. They did not have time for this delay. "First, because you owe me. And second, because Jedi make better friends than enemies. And you three can use friends, I think."

"That is true, since everyone despises us," Tup agreed sadly.

"All right, we'll help you," Cholly decided. "But wait until we're out of the building before you start your Jedi saber rattling."

Siri paced around the gravsled hauler, where the three had been loading droids. There was no exterior shell on a gravsled, just a platform and a windscreen. "But how can we hide? They'll see us at once."

"Don't you have a covered vehicle, like a skiff?" Adi asked.

"We could barely afford the gravsled," Cholly said. "But let me show you something. First, we have to unload the droids. Weez, Tup!"

Cholly, Weez, and Tup unloaded the handful

of droids that had already been loaded onto the gravsled. Then Cholly pressed a lever, and a hidden compartment in the gravsled slid open. It was cleverly disguised so that it appeared to be part of the vehicle's shell.

"We occasionally have the need for secrecy in transporting objects," Cholly explained.

"You mean smuggling," Siri said.

Adi peered into the opening. "Not much room, but I think we can all fit."

"You have to hide first. Then we load the droids," Weez explained.

"That means you have to unload the droids before we can get out," Siri observed with a frown.

Adi drummed her fingers on her holster. "Not the ideal situation. You'll have to offer to unload the droids as soon as we get inside."

Cholly did not look happy at this, but he nodded.

"What about programming the droids?" Adi asked. "Did Zan Arbor already give you instructions?"

Weez shook his head. "She's going to program them herself."

"Offer to do it. Make something up," Adi suggested. "Then sabotage them in some way. Better for us not to face twenty attack droids."

"We'll do our best," Cholly said. "You'd better get inside or we'll be late for our appointment."

Adi folded her long, elegant body into the small compartment and lay flat. Siri followed. Obi-Wan squeezed inside.

"Oof," Siri muttered. "Watch your elbows."

"I've got no place to put them," Obi-Wan responded.

"Quiet, you two," Adi said. "We won't be here for long."

Tup's cheerful face loomed above them. "I'm going to shut the panel now. Don't worry, there's plenty of ventilation."

"I hope so," Obi-Wan said softly as the panel slid closed just millimeters from their upturned faces. "I don't like having to put our trust in these three."

"Maybe because your friends seem so untrustworthy," Siri said.

"They aren't my friends," Obi-Wan muttered. Why did Siri always have to needle him?

For long minutes, they listened to Cholly, Weez, and Tup loading the droids, quarreling and fussing all the way.

"The more we fit, the more she'll take, if we're lucky!" Cholly exclaimed. "Don't put them in that way, Tup, you're taking up too much room."

"Woosh, I'm doing the best I can."

Adi sighed. "This is taking too long." She thumped on the top of the panel. "Hurry it up!" she shouted.

"Yes, yes, we're hurrying. Only a few minutes more," Cholly called.

Obi-Wan closed his eyes. Why was he always asked to be patient at the moment he was jumping out of his skin? Every second of delay was frustrating.

Adi spoke quietly. "Knowing Qui-Gon, I am sure that he has his own plan, Obi-Wan. We are not his only means of rescue."

"I am sure that he does as well," Obi-Wan said, grateful for Adi's words of reassurance.

"There is just one thing that troubles me," Adi murmured. "I only hope his plan does not collide with ours."

CHAPTER 3

For days, while he was stuck in the vapor-filled chamber, all Qui-Gon had wanted to do was get out and stretch his muscles. Thanks to his Padawan, he had been released from the chamber. But now, when he finally had his freedom, he found himself in an even tighter space — a ventilation shaft.

Jenna Zan Arbor had sealed herself into the room where she held the other prisoner. It had been a wise move. She knew that Qui-Gon would not dare to break in. She knew he would not gamble with the other being's life.

He could not use Obi-Wan's lightsaber to get through the door. He could not take any aggressive action. With a sensor in his body and one in the other prisoner's, both of them could be dead in an instant.

He would have to use stealth. He had found the ventilation shaft that ran through the ceiling. He had been crawling for what felt like a long time. He could not make a sound to alert her, and he had to be mindful of his direction as well. The various shafts were a maze. But if he was careful, he could wind up in the ceiling over Zan Arbor's head.

What then? Qui-Gon wondered. He could drop down on her from above. But what if the trigger for the sensor was concealed in her clothing? Even if it were somewhere on a console, could he persuade her to disable the sensors? Could he believe her if she said she had?

He didn't know the answers to those questions. But he could not wait outside the door, wondering what was going on inside.

He spied a vent ahead and carefully moved toward it. He lowered his face and peered through.

He was over the lab at last. He saw the top of Zan Arbor's head. The same kind of transparent chamber he had been kept in was in the middle of the room. It was filled with a cloudy gas, so he could not see the occupant.

Zan Arbor paced back and forth with short, quick steps. He recognized the angry movement. Something else had gone wrong.

"Do not think you can fool me," Zan Arbor said furiously. "I know you are willing yourself to die. You refuse to access the Force. I will not let that happen!" She strode over to a bank of equipment. "You want to die?" she asked shrilly. "Then know what it feels like to die!"

She turned an indicator knob. Qui-Gon did not know what she was doing. He could only imagine. Zan Arbor's goal was to break down the essential elements of the Force into something she could measure and control. Qui-Gon knew firsthand how ruthless she could be if her subject did not cooperate.

Hold on, he urged the prisoner silently.

She switched off the dial. "Well? Are you still so interested in dying? Now show me the Force!" Qui-Gon saw her send a sharp gaze to a chronometer to check the time. She was under some kind of pressure. Why?

"All right, then. If I cannot use you, you are just a liability. But I'll take all your blood *before* you die, just for being so uncooperative."

Her hand went for the dial again. It was time to act. Qui-Gon eased out Obi-Wan's lightsaber in one swift, practiced movement and reared back to kick through the vent.

But he checked himself just in time as an indicator buzzed and Zan Arbor hesitated. She pressed the communication button.

A voice blared, "Droid shipment."

"It's about time," she snarled.

She whirled and stalked from the room without another word. Qui-Gon settled back on his haunches, thinking. He could not release the prisoner until he knew that Zan Arbor was immobilized and unable to kill him. But any delay could seal his doom completely.

He was more trapped in his freedom than he'd been as a prisoner. What should he do?

CHAPTER 4

The gravsled ride was smooth while they were outside, but Cholly, Weez, and Tup had trouble maneuvering the craft through the narrow hallways of the lab. Each time Weez slammed into a wall, Obi-Wan, Astri, and Adi were thrown against one another, and the droids rattled noisily overhead.

"That's enough!" Obi-Wan recognized Zan Arbor's commanding tone. "Just stop! You can unload where you are."

With a last shuddering lurch, the repulsorlift engine lowered the gravsled to the floor.

"You can see that we only brought you the finest droids," Cholly said.

"These are your finest? I'd hate to see the rest."

"If you pardon my saying this, this *is* Simpla-12, ma'am," Weez said respectfully. "There isn't much choice to be had."

"I suppose so. Give me the CIP."

Obi-Wan tensed. The Central Intelligence Processor would program all the droids at once. Adi had instructed Cholly to try to program the droids himself. Would Zan Arbor allow him to do so?

"There's the matter of our fee . . ." Cholly said.

"Not until I'm sure these droids are operational."

"I can program them for you, ma'am," Cholly offered. "Part of our service. We aim to please!"

"It *pleases* me to program them myself. Give me the CIP." Apparently, Cholly hesitated, for Zan Arbor snapped, "Now!"

Adi let out a breath. Obi-Wan knew what she was thinking. It would have been easier if they didn't have the droids to contend with.

They heard a series of beeps and the sound of the droids' movements as they were activated.

"Follow my voice command only," Zan Arbor rapped out. "You will surround and protect me. We will be leaving from the launch pad on sublevel one in five minutes."

The droids beeped an affirmative response.

"Now unload them and I'll pay you the credits," Zan Arbor said to Cholly, Weez, and Tup. "Quickly!"

Overhead, Obi-Wan heard the noise of droids being unharnessed and wheeled off the gravsled platform.

"Watch out, Tup!" Cholly called. "You just —"

"I didn't! Weez —"

"Don't pull that way, push —"

"Not that way, over here, you idiots!" Zan Arbor shouted.

"I have it!"

"No, you don't!"

"I do!"

"No, you —"

A screeching noise and a great crash sent the gravsled shaking.

"Woosh," Tup said in a small voice. "Guess I didn't."

"Do it this way, Tup," Cholly shouted.

"If you didn't shout like that, I wouldn't be so confused," Tup dithered. "Just let me —"

The gravsled rose slightly in the air. There was a crash.

"Turn off the engine! You're tipping it!" Zan Arbor screamed. "The droids are falling —"

"Gibbertz and ham, let me —"

"Don't touch that!" Cholly and Weez screamed at the same moment.

It was too late. Tup hit the hidden lever, and the compartment door sprang open. Adi, Obi-

Wan, and Siri tumbled out onto the floor. They rolled away from the repulsorlift engine as the gravsled hovered a few inches above the floor.

"Jedi!" Zan Arbor screamed.

Most of the droids had been unloaded, and the Jedi had landed right in the midst of them. The gravsled hemmed them in against the wall.

"Attack!" Zan Arbor shouted, backing away from the gravsled. "Shoot to kill!"

Tup's face went white, and he dropped to the floor. Cholly and Weez jumped off the gravsled. The droids wheeled, positioning the blasters built in their arms.

Adi, Obi-Wan, and Siri reached for their lightsabers. Blaster fire erupted from every direction. They were caught in a deadly crossfire.

CHAPTER 5

Qui-Gon had just decided to go through the vent and rescue the prisoner when he heard the sound of blaster fire. That could mean only one thing. A Jedi team had arrived.

With one smooth motion he cut through the shaft with Obi-Wan's lightsaber and dropped to the floor. Then he accessed the lab door and burst out into the hallway, racing toward the sound.

He rounded the corner and swept the battle with one glance. The Jedi were faced with twenty armed droids. Obi-Wan had no lightsaber, just a vibroblade. Jenna Zan Arbor stood in the opposite corner, watching. The sneer on her face announced that she was confident of victory.

Qui-Gon watched for a few extra seconds in order to grasp Adi's strategy. Even while she mowed down droids, she protected Obi-Wan from the worst of the fire. She was using a series of short, fast combinations designed to obscure the fact that she was steadily making progress toward Jenna Zan Arbor and the hallway to the rest of the lab.

Obi-Wan was using the vibroblade effectively, but it was no match for blaster fire. Qui-Gon decided, even as he leaped, that his job would be to protect his Padawan, leaving Adi free to go after Zan Arbor.

A flash of joyful relief lit Obi-Wan's face as he saw Qui-Gon sail toward him. His moment of distraction was smoothly covered by Adi, who in a lightning strike took out a droid who aimed a blaster at Obi-Wan. Qui-Gon came down, knocking out two droids as he landed and whirling to deflect fire from a third. He was surprised to find that although he had succeeded, his reaction times were slow. He could not trust his body to move quickly. The days of captivity had taken a worse toll on him than he'd thought.

Qui-Gon received a sense of satisfaction when he saw Zan Arbor's expression turn from smugness to alarm. She knew now that the tide would turn against her. With a sharp command, she ordered four droids to surround her. Her back was to the wall.

Qui-Gon accessed the Force to help him overcome his body's weakness. He deftly attacked, slashing through the metal bodies of the droids while Siri whirled and dived, her lightsaber a blur. The young girl's footwork was impeccable. Obi-Wan was hampered by his vibroblade but kept up a steady attack, sweat pouring down his face.

There were only five droids left, excluding the guard around Zan Arbor. Qui-Gon did not need to look at Adi for confirmation as he drove the droids toward her. They would catch them in a pincer movement. Understanding his intent, both Siri and Obi-Wan moved to flank him.

The plan would have worked perfectly if Tup hadn't chosen that moment to make a break for safety. Hearing a slight lull in blaster fire, he scrambled out from underneath the hovering gravsled and dashed toward the hallway.

Unfortunately, he crashed into two droids, driving them back toward Obi-Wan. The droids wheeled and raised their arms toward Tup, prepared to blast him.

"G-giberbtz and h-ham!" Tup screamed.

Obi-Wan was closest. He accessed the Force and leaped, coming down with both feet hitting the two droids squarely. The droids wobbled and the blaster fire went awry. Obi-Wan landed and swung his vibroblade at the first droid. It raised its blaster toward Obi-Wan.

Qui-Gon reached out a hand to use the Force to send the droid flying. Nothing happened. Adi reversed direction to neatly slice the second droid in two.

"Zan Arbor," Siri said tersely.

Jenna Zan Arbor had taken advantage of the distraction to slip out from behind the droids that were guarding her and dash down the hall. She was just disappearing into a turbolift.

"There are stairs," Qui-Gon told Adi. "Second door on the left."

"Siri and I will follow," Adi told him, already starting off.

"We'll see to the prisoner," Qui-Gon said, signaling to Obi-Wan.

He raced down the hallway, his Padawan by his side. They burst into the lab. Qui-Gon strode to the cloud-filled chamber and cut through the material with Obi-Wan's lightsaber. The transparent material peeled back and gas escaped in a vaporous cloud.

The chamber was empty.

"We have been fooled," Qui-Gon said quietly.

"Maybe Noor R'aya is in the other lab," Obi-Wan suggested.

Qui-Gon looked startled. "Noor R'aya? The prisoner was a Jedi?"

"Adi thinks so."

"She said I did not know him, but I was close

to him," Qui-Gon murmured. "Of course that is so. Every Jedi shares a bond."

"We should head for the launching pad," Obi-Wan said. "Zan Arbor said it is on sub-level one."

"In that case," Qui-Gon said, "I am sure it is not. Come, Padawan."

He did not know for certain if he was right, but he had come to know the turnings of Zan Arbor's mind, the way she strategized. She would enjoy flipping the situation so that the Jedi were in the opposite place of where they should be when she made her escape.

So instead of heading for sub-level one, Qui-Gon headed for the roof.

He did not trust the turbolift. No doubt she would have sabotaged it. He took the stairs, Obi-Wan at his heels.

They burst out onto the roof just in time to see Jenna Zan Arbor's craft rise in the air. They saw the body of Noor R'aya in the seat next to her. He was slumped over as if he were too weak to raise his head. She smiled and waved a split second before the craft shot into the upper atmosphere.

They had lost her again.

CHAPTER 6

Obi-Wan waited while the Jedi medic, Winna Di Uni, attended to Qui-Gon. She located the sensor implanted in his bloodstream and carefully extracted it. While he waited, Obi-Wan searched the lab and located Qui-Gon's lightsaber. It was a great pleasure for him to place it back in his Master's hands.

"How is Didi?" Obi-Wan asked Winna.

She smiled. "On the mend. He is already suggesting better ways to prepare his meals."

Qui-Gon groaned. "Whatever you do, don't listen to him." Didi's abilities as a chef were dismal.

Winna touched Qui-Gon's shoulder. "You've been through a trauma, Qui-Gon. Your body has not recovered fully. I suppose it would be fruitless for me to tell you to take it easy."

Qui-Gon winced as he slid off the examination table. "Not until we find Noor."

Obi-Wan saw the signs of fatigue he had missed in his joy to have his Master well and safe. Jenna Zan Arbor had drained Qui-Gon's body of blood. She had kept him confined for long periods of time. His skin looked pale and his face drawn. The experience had weakened him.

"Are you sure you shouldn't return to the Temple?" he asked Qui-Gon in a low voice.

"No," Qui-Gon said sharply.

Adi and Siri strode into the room.

"We've checked all the computer files," Adi said crisply. "There's no indication of where she might go next."

"There was an assistant, Nil," Qui-Gon said.

"Not anymore," Siri said. "We found him in one of the storage rooms. A lethal injection, we think."

"He was a liability," Qui-Gon said. He turned away. "She will stop at nothing."

"Yes, that's why we must find her," Adi agreed quietly.

Cholly, Weez, and Tup peered around the corner.

"If you're no longer in need of our services, we thought we would go back to our poverty-stricken but basically safe existence," Cholly offered.

"She had the credits in her hand," Weez said. "If only Tup hadn't started the engine —"

"Or knocked over the droids —"

"Woosh, everything is all my fault, all the time, forever," Tup complained.

"Yes, it is," Cholly and Weez said together.

Qui-Gon's comlink signaled. "It's Tahl."

A miniature hologram of Tahl appeared before them. "I am relieved to hear that you all are safe and that Didi will recover," she said. "The Force is with us. Winna, how is Qui-Gon?"

"Fine," Qui-Gon said tersely.

"Excuse me, did I ask you that question?" Tahl demanded. She was one of the few Jedi who was brave enough to challenge Qui-Gon, let alone tease him. "Winna?"

"He has undergone a great trauma," Winna said. "My best advice would be to return to the Temple, but I know he is needed. There will be no lasting damage. He just needs rest and food."

"Then you will release him on a mission?" Tahl asked.

"Release me?" Qui-Gon thundered irritably. "Am I still a captive?"

"No, you are a stubborn Jedi who might push himself beyond a limit his body cannot handle," Tahl answered.

"I see no danger to him," Winna said reluctantly. "I have seen how quickly Qui-Gon is able to recover his strength. As long as he has been honest with me about how he is feeling and not covering up any weakness."

Qui-Gon glared at her.

"I'm sure he was covering them up," Tahl said crisply. "However, we must pursue Jenna Zan Arbor. The Council wishes the two Jedi teams to join together to find Noor."

Obi-Wan glanced at Siri. So he would have to work with her again, side by side. He hoped she had learned a little more humility since their last mission.

"I have news for you, Obi-Wan," Tahl said. "And you will not like it. Nor do I. As soon as she was assured that Didi would make a full recovery, Astri left the Temple. She has gone off to pursue Ona Nobis in hopes of getting the reward."

"Astri is no match for Ona Nobis!" Obi-Wan cried in surprise.

Tahl sighed. "I know this. Yet there is nothing the Jedi can do. She does not wish our protection any longer. We cannot force it."

Obi-Wan felt frustration and worry battle within him. Yet he knew Tahl was right. The Jedi did not impose protection. And his mission was to find Jenna Zan Arbor.

"Adi and Qui-Gon, contact me when you decide on your next move," Tahl finished.

"Meanwhile, I am coordinating the search for Zan Arbor's ship."

"It's a big galaxy," Qui-Gon said.

"Then I'd better get going," Tahl said, and signed off.

More and more, Obi-Wan had grown to appreciate having Tahl as a liaison within the Temple. When they rescued a blinded Tahl from Melida/Daan, he had never expected how important she would become in their lives, as well as their missions.

"It's been a swell adventure, but we must be going," Cholly said.

Adi turned to them. "We are grateful for your help. We regret that you were caught in a battle."

Weez waved his hand. "It was nothing."

"Especially when it was over," Tup said, blowing out a relieved breath.

Giving a last bow and a quick wave from Tup, the three hurried from the lab. No doubt they were anxious to get away from the Jedi, Obi-Wan thought. It was no wonder that Cholly, Weez, and Tup were such hopeless criminals. Their courage did not match their greed. At the first sign of trouble, they ran.

Qui-Gon turned to Adi. "Did you and Siri discover anything that could help us while you were investigating Noor's disappearance?"

"I don't think so," Adi said thoughtfully, "but let me tell you a little about him. Noor had a deep connection to the Force that led him to choose a life of meditation when he became an elder. He left the Temple and returned to his home planet, Sorl, where he planned to live in quiet seclusion. He built a simple home in the foothills of the great mountain range of Cragh. Things did not turn out quite the way he expected."

"As they seldom do," Qui-Gon noted.

Adi nodded. "When Siri and I reached Sorl, we discovered that to pass the time, Noor had begun to craft small landscapes out of stone, sticks, and vegetation. He made small animals and figures and placed them in these imaginary landscapes, places he had seen over his long life. We saw them in the yards and fields surrounding his home. They were charming. Beautiful."

"Ah," Qui-Gon said. "And they began to attract some attention."

Adi smiled. "From the children. They began to come by to watch Noor work. He began to make toys for them. Soon he was involved in the life of the community. His life of seclusion became a life of engagement."

"'Life surprises you. Accept the gift,'" Qui-Gon recited. It was a Jedi saying.

"So you see, all we know about Noor will not help us here," Adi finished. "I think we must concentrate on Jenna Zan Arbor. Yet so much of her life is a mystery. . . ."

Obi-Wan's comlink began to signal him. He stepped off a few paces to accept the communication.

"My name is Ivo Muna and I am a medic at the Med Center on Sorrus," a voice said. "I was given your name by Astri Oddo —"

"Is Astri all right?"

"I am afraid she is not. An accident — she is not conscious, I'm afraid. She gave me your name before she passed out. She asked you to come here. Yinn La Hi is the capital city of Sorrus, in the system of —"

"Yes, I know where it is," Obi-Wan interrupted. "Thank you. If she awakens, tell her I am on my way."

He cut the communication. The others had stopped talking and were listening to him. He met Qui-Gon's gaze.

"I have to," he said.

Qui-Gon frowned, but Obi-Wan knew it was a frown of concentration, not displeasure.

"Yes," he said. "We cannot leave Astri on Sorrus alone. But the chances of finding Zan Arbor and Noor diminish with every moment of delay. Adi and I will remain here to begin the search. You go with Siri to Sorrus and escort Astri back to the Temple, if she is able to travel. We'll either meet back at the Temple or tell you where you must come." Qui-Gon seemed to recall that he was supposed to collaborate with Adi. He turned to her. "Do you agree?"

There was a beat before Adi responded. "I agree." She turned to Siri. "I am sending you alone with Obi-Wan. This means I am trusting you not to engage with the bounty hunter Ona Nobis or pursue any lead unless you contact me."

"The same goes for you, Obi-Wan," Qui-Gon told him. "Ona Nobis will have revenge on her mind if she knows you are on Sorrus. Keep a low profile. Do not cause any disturbance. And contact us immediately after you see Astri. Now let's find you some transport."

CHAPTER 7

Sorrus was a large planet in a busy system, and it was easy to find a hauler making a direct run. After landing at the capital city of Yinn La Hi, Obi-Wan and Siri thanked the pilot.

"Now we'll have trouble," Obi-Wan said to Siri as they exited the busy landing platform area. "There are no signs in the cities on Sorrus, and we have to find our way to the Med Center."

"Why don't we just ask someone?" Siri asked.

"We won't get very far. Sorrusians don't like strangers."

"You make everything so hard, Obi-Wan," Siri scoffed. "You just have to be polite." She approached a Sorrusian couple, their arms filled with produce from the open-air market.

"Excuse me," Siri said. "Can you tell us where the Med Center is located?"

The couple gave her a blank stare, then moved on, chatting in Sorrusian as if Siri didn't exist.

"That was rude," Siri said. She hailed a young Sorrusian who was strolling by, his hands tucked into his tunic pockets.

"Excuse me. My companion and I are strangers here. We need directions to —"

The young man wheeled about and walked away from them.

"Do you believe me now?" Obi-Wan asked. "Are you sure you were polite enough?"

"They're positively paranoid," Siri grumbled, running a hand through her hair. "How are we going to find the place?"

"The center should be fairly large, and on a main street," Obi-Wan said, his eyes scanning the street ahead. "And the pilot said he thought it was close to the city center. It should be right around here."

After only a few minutes of quick walking, Obi-Wan and Siri found the complex. Yinn La Hi was a teeming city, and the Med Center was spread out over a large area. Soon it would take up even more space. A new wing was under construction.

"Now we'll have to get someone to tell us where Astri is," Siri observed as they walked through the doors into a gleaming atrium that swarmed with Sorrusians.

"Why don't you try?" Obi-Wan asked. "You did so well earlier."

Siri gave him an irritated glance. Obi-Wan walked ahead to the reception desk.

"I received a message from Ivo Muna that Astri Oddo was brought here for treatment."

The Sorrusian clerk behind the desk said nothing, just continued tapping on the keyboard.

Obi-Wan leaned over the desk in frustration. He spoke clearly and insistently. "My friend is hurt and I must see her!"

The clerk looked up at him warily. "What did you say your name was?"

"Obi-Wan Kenobi."

A spark of recognition lit the clerk's blank gaze. "Ah, I was told to expect you. Please see Medic Rai Unlu. He is waiting for you over there."

Obi-Wan saw a short, slender Sorrusian standing by a pillar. He wore a med smock and carried a small datapad. Obi-Wan and Siri hurried over, and Obi-Wan introduced himself.

"Oh, yes, Astri Oddo. Sad case. We do not know how she received her injuries," the Sorrusian doctor said gravely. "Let me check to see her status." He pressed several keys. "Ah. She has regained consciousness. That is a good sign."

"I must see her," Obi-Wan said.

"Of course. But first you must fill out registry information. All foreigners must do so on Sorrus. You will have to go to Wing A, Level 27, Room 2245X. Astri is in Wing M, at the opposite end of the complex. After you fill out the information, you can ask for directions to her room at the Registry Office."

"Good luck," Siri muttered.

"But that will take too much time!" Obi-Wan objected. "I need to see her now."

"Why don't I fill out the papers while Obi-Wan visits Astri?" Siri suggested. "Would that be all right?"

Rai Unlu looked uncertain. "It is not procedure —"

"I've come so far to see her," Obi-Wan said persuasively. "And she's been badly hurt."

"All right," Rai Unlu said, looking around furtively. "But don't tell anyone. I will take you to Astri. Your companion can follow signs to Wing A. There will be signs to the Registry Office from there."

Siri nodded. "Good luck, Obi-Wan. I will come to Astri's room as soon as I am finished."

Siri strode off, and Rai Unlu beckoned to Obi-Wan. "This way."

Obi-Wan followed him from the soaring

atrium through a series of gleaming corridors. They stepped onto a moving ramp and were swept through wing after wing.

At last, Rai Unlu stepped off the ramp at Wing L. "We must walk from here."

They walked quickly through the wing, past the closed doors of the ward. Then they came to a sign that read NO ADMITTANCE.

"Restricted ward for foreigners," Rai Unlu explained, hurrying through.

To Obi-Wan's surprise, they stepped through a doorway into a partially completed hallway. Small gravsleds with construction materials littered the corridor, and through the open gridwork of the ceiling Obi-Wan saw ducts and wires.

"The Med Center is very crowded. We had to put her in the new wing," Rai Unlu said.

"But it's not finished," Obi-Wan said, stepping over a pail full of rivets.

"She is still getting the best care," Rai Unlu assured him. "Sorrus has the best med facilities in the galaxy."

It was a claim Obi-Wan had heard on other worlds. Had Astri been shuttled to this far wing because she was a stranger? Sorrusians weren't noted for their hospitality, but he expected a more sterile environment.

"She is just through here, third door on your left," Rai Unlu said. "I must return. I have an emergency."

"Wait," Obi-Wan said.

"Sorry, must go," Rai Unlu said. "I'm being signaled. Emergency!"

He turned and almost ran down the hall. Obi-Wan's growing wariness turned to concern. He felt a disturbance in the Force that alarmed him. Prepared for anything now, his hand went to his lightsaber hilt.

Cautiously, he opened the third door on the left. Instead of a private room, he found himself in a partially built hospital ward. There were beams overhead and a durasteel frame. Only two walls had been constructed.

He just had time to see a shadow flicker, nothing more. Obi-Wan stepped back, lightsaber activated, as the bounty hunter Ona Nobis suddenly flew from a beam overhead straight toward him.

CHAPTER 8

Obi-Wan had captured her laser whip back on Simpla-12. He was not happy to see that she had replaced it. It danced toward him, an arc of supple, lethal light. He struck out at the whip before it reached him. The two lasers tangled and smoked.

He could not move as fast as Ona Nobis. That, he remembered. He could not defeat her with quickness. She was an astoundingly agile fighter with lightning-fast moves. Her mind was quick as well. She always had surprises up her sleeve.

Cleverness. Acrobatics. Cunning. Flexibility. She had everything he had been taught was important in battle. His adversary did not have the Force, but she might have the advantage.

In this partially enclosed space, he was too vulnerable. He must get out in the open. Obi-Wan drove Ona Nobis back with a furious flurry of moves, forcing her to concentrate on defending herself. When she was slightly off balance he vaulted to the top of the unfinished wall. Balancing for a moment, he leaped down into the construction site.

Here there were obstacles — gravsleds, drills, large piles of metal poles, blocks of stone, a durasteel skeleton of the exterior walls of the wing, a deep, muddy pit. Yet he could use them for defense and attack. Here the Force could help him.

The whip snaked to the top of the wall behind him, curling around an exposed rod. A moment later Ona Nobis used it to haul herself up. Her head swiveled toward him in the black visor she wore to conceal her eyes. Then she leaped down, landing lightly, already furling the whip for another attack.

Her lips curled back from her teeth. "I've been waiting for this," she said.

He was ready. Every sense was alert, every particle of his being focused on the battle ahead. He had to be. The trick was to get her close. From a distance, she used the whip to devastating effect. If he were closer, she would have no room to maneuver.

The perfect attack begins with your attention. Every pebble can be an obstacle or an opportunity. Hone your focus. Add speed, timing, strat-

egy, surprise. Do not forget the Force is with you.

Obi-Wan leaped to his opponent's left side. He used a technique Qui-Gon called "false attack." He knew he would not win with this strategy, but he did not mean to. He wanted to draw her forward toward him.

His lightsaber whirled and blurred as he moved, deflecting her curling whip with its spiked edge. He saw her hand move toward the blaster strapped to her hip and he blocked it with a flurry of moves so fast she had to concentrate to keep up.

The ground was treacherous with mud and debris, but he used the Force to aid every step. He leaped on a pyramid of stone blocks and used the momentum to flip in midair and come at her left. Instead of stepping backward, she stepped forward, an unexpected move for anyone but Ona Nobis.

Good. He had expected it, planned for it.

He twisted in midair, adding momentum to his leap. He landed behind her. Now her back was to a sinkhole filled with mud and water. There was no telling if it was shallow or meters deep.

He drove her relentlessly backward. He saw her lip curl with anger as she flicked the whip, sending it within millimeters of his flesh. He slashed downward. The lasers tangled with a buzzing noise.

Suddenly the blaster was in her hand. He had only caught a blur of movement as she reached for it. But he was ready, his lightsaber spinning in a continuous arc to deflect the fire. The Force surged in him, making every movement sure.

But he could not concentrate on everything at once. He lost his connection to the ground. Chips of stone lay around the muddy surface, and they were slippery. His foot slid and he lost his balance. He caught himself before he fell but his loss of concentration cost him.

She moved to his right and charged, firing as she went. Obi-Wan slid on the slippery stones, struggling to regain his footing as he deflected the furious round of fire, twisting his body. He felt the rush of air as the whip snaked around him.

For the first time, he was seriously worried. He was outmatched and he knew it. He did not have Qui-Gon's perfect mastery of the Force. And he could not meet the dual challenge of the whip and the blaster. He could not get close enough to disarm her, and he doubted he would be lucky enough to capture the whip a second time. He had only managed to do so back on Simpla-12 because Astri had barreled down on Ona Nobis in a gravsled.

Doubt is your first enemy. How many times had he heard that in class? Yet he knew deep within that this doubt was justified. With a whip as well as a blaster, she could keep him running while she remained still. Sooner or later he would tire. He saw how much he depended on Qui-Gon during a battle. He could pick up on Qui-Gon's strategy, but he could not formulate it himself. He would put up a good fight, maybe even wound her, if he were lucky to get close enough. But she would win. She knew this territory well and she had set the trap. He had walked right into it.

All of these calculations roared through Obi-Wan's mind even as he regained his footing and faked a pass at Ona Nobis, forcing her to retreat a few steps. He knew it was a temporary victory.

The hardest decision, Qui-Gon had told him once, *is to walk away.* He had not understood that. Until now. It went against everything he'd learned about battle, everything he was as a Jedi.

Or did it? The mission was his first concern.

Ona Nobis was not part of his mission. As far as they knew, she had no connection to Jenna Zan Arbor now. She had picked a fight solely for revenge.

Which meant there was no reason to fight.

Behind Ona Nobis, tall girders framed a wall

of the wing. He needed a few seconds, that was all.

Concentrating all his will, he reached out a hand toward a fusioncutter lying on the ground. He felt the Force move, and the fusioncutter slid along the mud and then flew with sudden momentum straight toward Ona Nobis.

Surprised, she slashed at it with her whip. Obi-Wan felt the power in his legs as he leaped straight over her head toward the girder above. He landed, slipping just a bit from the mud on his boots. But he knew he would regain his balance. He bent his legs and leaped again, this time to a higher girder.

Far below, the whip snaked toward him. It could not reach him as he leaped to the next high girder. From here, he leapfrogged his way down, out of her reach at the far side of the site. Her howl of rage rang in his ears as he raced away.

CHAPTER 9

Siri was waiting for Obi-Wan back in the atrium, her vivid blue eyes snapping with impatience.

"This place is crazy," she said before Obi-Wan could speak. "There is no Wing M. Or if there is, I can't find it, and would you care to make a bet on how helpful the Sorrusians were? Plus, Astri isn't even registered here. I went to Wing A, and they had never heard of her. So then I asked about Rai Unlu. Get this — they've never heard of him, either. Or at least that's what they tell me. I don't know whether they're lying, or I'm trapped in a nightmare." For the first time, Siri noticed Obi-Wan's mud-splattered tunic and dirty face. "Did you fall in a puddle?"

"I had a run-in with Ona Nobis," Obi-Wan said. "This whole thing was a setup. I don't think Astri's here at all. Ona Nobis lured us here to get revenge on me."

"So what happened?" Siri asked, instantly poised for action.

Obi-Wan thought the decision to leave the battle was hard. He hadn't thought ahead to telling Siri. This was harder.

"We fought. I left," he said.

Siri looked incredulous. "You ran away?"

Obi-Wan felt his annoyance rise. Why did Siri have to put it that way? He struggled not to let his anger show. The best way to tell her what happened was not to offer excuses.

"I was outmatched this time." The words seemed to come out smoothly, but they felt as though they'd been torn from his throat.

Siri opened her mouth, then snapped it shut. Obviously, there were many things she wanted to say. Just as obviously, Adi had taught her well. For once, she kept her thoughts to herself.

Yet the expression on her face spoke more clearly than anything she could have said. Siri could not understand leaving the scene of a battle. She could not imagine a situation in which she would give up. She had not been in as many battles as Obi-Wan. She was more used to the training rooms at the Temple, where she had usually been the winner. When she had lost, she had bowed to her opponent with grace. Then she beat them in the next encounter.

She did not yet realize that even for the best Jedi, there were battles that could not be won. Qui-Gon had taught Obi-Wan that. As skilled a fighter as he was, Qui-Gon knew that surprises in battle came often. You could train for them, but you could not predict them. Sometimes you had to cut your losses.

He wanted to tell Siri this, but Siri would not listen. She liked to find things out her own way. And you did not go to her for a sympathetic ear.

"We'd better contact Qui-Gon and Adi," Obi-Wan said, turning away.

They found a secluded place to talk in the gardens in the center of the med complex. Qui-Gon's calm voice came through the comlink, and Obi-Wan quickly described what had occurred.

There was a pause. "You did well, Padawan," Qui-Gon said. Obi-Wan felt some of the tension inside his body uncurl. Qui-Gon understood his decision, at least. "Ona Nobis is only a distraction for us now. But this news distresses me. Astri has not checked in with Tahl. If Ona Nobis used her as a lure, that means she must know that Astri is on Sorrus. She must know where she is."

"Siri and I can look for her —"

"No," Qui-Gon interrupted. "Hard as it is, I

must agree with Tahl. Astri has made her own decision. She has not asked for our help."

"But —"

"Obi-Wan, listen to me. Do nothing. Tahl, Adi, and I will discuss this. You and Siri return to the Temple immediately."

It was Qui-Gon's sternest voice. Obi-Wan tucked his comlink back into his belt. Reluctantly, he turned to Siri. "We'll be able to hitch a ride from the main landing platform."

She nodded. She was silent on the walk back to the landing platform. Obi-Wan did not know what to say, either. He and Siri had formed a bond during their adventure on Kegan. He had liked her spirit and humor and had depended on her courage. Obviously, they still had a distance to travel before they became real friends. He felt a sudden sharp ache for his friend Bant, who would never let him feel like a coward for leaving the scene of a battle. She would trust his judgment. Siri only trusted her own.

When they got to the landing platform, Obi-Wan looked for a hauler on a direct run to Coruscant. The first pilot he approached refused, but pointed to another pilot nearby.

"Donny Buc is about to make a run. He'll probably let you hitch a ride. He's been laid up for repairs for a day, but he's ready to roll."

Obi-Wan saw a pilot squatting near his ship,

drinking a carton of muja juice. He signaled to Siri and approached him.

"Sure, I can always find room for Jedi," the pilot said. "Are you ready to leave now?"

"Yes." Obi-Wan had a sudden impulse. "By any chance, has someone else tried to hitch a ride earlier today? She's tall and has a shaved head —"

"Sure, I remember her," the pilot said, taking a last gulp of juice. He wore a tattered leather helmet and sported a short black beard. "Her and some of her friends were looking for transport to the far desert."

"Friends?" Obi-Wan asked, puzzled.

"Three of them," the pilot said. "They kept quarreling about how much they were willing to pay. Wouldn't listen to a word the girl said."

Obi-Wan closed his eyes. "Their names wouldn't be Cholly, Weez, and Tup, by any chance?"

"That was them!" the pilot chortled. "What a bunch of chuckleheads."

"Did you transport them to Arra?" Obi-Wan asked. That was no doubt where she was headed.

He shook his head. "Couldn't swing it, I had repairs to wait for. I told them to take an air taxi. Saw them heading toward the taxi platform."

Obi-Wan drew Siri aside. "Now we can be

pretty sure that Astri is here. We've got to check this out. It won't take long. If this pilot will take us to Arra first, we can pick up Astri and bring her back with us to the Temple."

"But Qui-Gon and Adi want us to return immediately."

"That was before we knew for sure that Astri was here," Obi-Wan argued. "We know that Ona Nobis is here in the capital city, so we won't be in danger. We can swing by, pick up Astri, and head straight for the Temple."

Siri shook her head. "We are wasting time, Obi-Wan. I don't understand why we had to rescue Astri in the first place. Why is Qui-Gon bending the rules for this girl? She isn't a Jedi. She can't lead us to Jenna Zan Arbor. This is a distraction."

"She needs us," Obi-Wan said. "Qui-Gon has known her since she was a child. If she is in danger and we can help, we must. Your Master sent you here to Sorrus, just as much as Qui-Gon did."

Siri gave him a stony glance. "Adi did not want to. She went along with Qui-Gon out of loyalty."

"Then you should do the same for me."

Siri said nothing for a long moment. She squinted into the distance, as if counting the tall buildings in Yinn La Hi. "All right," she said finally. "But we must not delay more than a few hours."

Obi-Wan quickly made a deal with the pilot.

"All right. It's only a little out of my way," the pilot said. "I wouldn't want your friend to get herself in trouble."

They boarded the transport and took off. Obi-Wan's impatience made the flight seem to last forever. As the pilot slowed the engines and began landing procedures, a blinking warning light suddenly lit on the panel.

"Well, eclipse my moon, there's that same problem," he said, hitting the panel with an angry fist. "That mechanic didn't fix my problem after all. Maybe I shouldn't have bought that discount part. I'm going to have to drop you and head back to Yinn."

"But we have to get to Coruscant!" Siri exclaimed.

"Well, you can come back with me, if you want," Donny Buc said genially, slowing the engines further. "Don't worry, we'll make it back to the landing platform. Should be a couple of hours, that's all."

Siri groaned in frustration. "I don't believe this! We could have been halfway to Coruscant by now."

"Sorry, little girl," Buc said cheerfully. "The

hyperdrive's busted. Lucky we made this detour so I can get back to the mechanic. You could hitch another ride from Yinn, I guess. But nobody else was making a run near Coruscant today."

Siri bristled at being called "little girl." "I don't like any of these options."

"It will only mean a few hours delay," Obi-Wan said.

"Maybe less," Buc said, shrugging.

"We might as well get off here," Obi-Wan said to Siri. "We can look for Astri while we wait. You've come this far."

Siri pressed her lips together. She gave a short, angry nod.

"All right, drop us here," he told Donny Buc. "We'll be at the landing platform in two hours."

"Make it an hour and a half. I feel lucky."

Donny Buc swooped in for a bumpy landing. They scrambled off the craft and he made a wobbly takeoff back to Yinn.

Siri and Obi-Wan were hit with a blast of hot wind.

"All I can say is, he'd better come back," Siri grumbled.

Obi-Wan led the way through the sand. He was grateful to Siri for agreeing to stop. She may have been disdainful of him back at the

Med Center, she might be angry now, but one thing he could say about Siri — she was loyal.

They struck out over the dunes. Obi-Wan saw no sign of the tribe or Astri with her three companions. But up ahead, he caught the glint of metal.

"Siri, look."

She shaded her eyes with her hand. "It's an air taxi," she said. "Come on."

They ran ahead, the sand sucking at their footsteps.

The air taxi was settled into the sand, but did not appear to have crashed. As they got closer, Obi-Wan saw a bundle of clothing in the front seat.

His heartbeat tripped. It was not a bundle of clothes. It was a pilot. He'd been strangled.

CHAPTER 10

Barely breathing, Obi-Wan walked closer to search the rest of the ship. He braced himself for the sight of Astri's lifeless body. But how could you brace yourself for something like that?

The air taxi was empty except for the pilot.

"What should we do, Obi-Wan?" Siri asked in a hushed voice. She anxiously scanned the area around them. "Do you think Ona Nobis killed the pilot?"

"I have no doubt of it."

"What do you think happened to Astri? Do you think . . ."

"I don't know," Obi-Wan said uneasily.

"Maybe she's hiding. Is there anywhere you can think to look?"

"Yes," Obi-Wan said. He tried to ignore the foreboding that was gathering inside him.

"There is one place. When Astri and I were here, the local tribe led us to the bounty hunter's hideout."

He led Siri along the sheer rock wall that circled the canyon. When he got to a sharp turning, he stopped.

"Put your hood up," he advised. "The wind will get very strong after we turn the corner. Whatever you do, don't lose sight of me."

Siri nodded, drawing her hood over her face. He did the same.

They turned the corner into a howling wind. Pellets of sand peppered any exposed skin. Obi-Wan kept one hand on the wall so that he would not get lost. He could only see a meter or two ahead.

He dropped to his knees, motioning to Siri to follow. His fingers trailed along the rock, looking for the opening to the bounty hunter's hideout.

It was a relief to enter the narrow opening of the cave. He could not stand, but the cool sand under his fingers felt good. He shook out his cloak and brushed the sand from his face and hair.

"The cave opens up just ahead. We'll be able to stand," he told Siri in a whisper. He was fairly sure that Ona Nobis wasn't here, but he was prepared to meet her if she was. This time, he would have Siri by his side.

He crawled along the cool, damp sand, feeling his way in the darkness. He saw the small opening ahead and squeezed through. Immediately the air felt different and he knew he was in a larger open space. The blackness turned gray. He waited a moment, then lit his glow rod.

Astri sat against one wall with Cholly, Weez, and Tup. They were tethered together, their wrists and ankles tightly bound. Gags were stuffed in their mouths. Astri's eyes went wide.

"Don't worry, it's me," Obi-Wan called, in case they had trouble seeing him.

"Mmmmfff!" Astri struggled against the gag. Cholly beat his feet on the floor of the cave.

"All right, I'm coming," Obi-Wan said, hurrying toward them. He reached toward Astri's gag even as she attempted to talk.

"Trap!" Astri exhaled the word as Obi-Wan removed the gag.

"Wh —" Obi-Wan's question was cut off as he heard a loud rushing noise behind him.

He turned and ran past Siri to the opening. He dropped flat and pushed forward, but it was too late. Sand and rocks were pouring down from overhead, piling up against the cave entrance. There was nothing he could do. Larger rocks spilled down, wedging in against one another tightly. In only moments, the cave opening was sealed and they were buried alive.

CHAPTER 11

Obi-Wan crawled back into the larger cave. He wiped the dust out of his eyes and reached for his comlink.

It didn't work.

"Siri?"

She shook her head. "Mine doesn't work, either."

Astri ran her hands over the stubble that was beginning to grow back on her bare skull. "I'm sorry, Obi-Wan. She left us here to die, but she was hoping you'd find us. When you crawled through, you tripped a slow-acting lever that deposited all that debris."

Obi-Wan nodded. He felt foolish for once again walking into a trap. He had never told Qui-Gon about Ona Nobis's hideout. There hadn't been time. He had told Tahl, but he hadn't given her coordinates. Everything had happened too fast. And now no one knew where they were.

Siri had freed Cholly, Weez, and Tup. Tup groaned as he stretched his legs. "I'm so hungry."

"You won't be for long," Weez said.

Tup brightened. "There's food?"

"No, idiot. Because soon we'll be dead," Weez snarled.

Tup paled. "You don't have to be so negative. Woosh. We're with Jedi. They can do anything."

Cholly had crawled forward to peer through the opening to the cave-in. "They can't tunnel through a rock," he said.

"You're not dead yet," Siri told them. "Come on, Obi-Wan, let's see if we can cut through those rocks with our lightsabers."

Obi-Wan followed Siri back into the narrow portion of the cave. They crawled forward. There was just enough room to crouch side by side. They activated their lightsabers and sliced through the rocks.

The rocks crumbled into sand, which filled up the spaces, packing the landslide even tighter.

"This isn't going to work," Obi-Wan said. He sat back and deactivated his lightsaber. He wiped the dirt off his face with his sleeve. "Now you get to say 'I told you so.'"

Siri sat down beside him. She dusted the sand off her tunic with her hands. "If you say that again," she muttered, "I'll hit you. There's got to be another way. Maybe she has tools in the cave."

"I'm sure she removed them. Ona Nobis plans for everything."

With a grunt, Siri flipped over and began to crawl back to the cave. "Maybe she doesn't know it's a tool."

Intrigued, Obi-Wan crawled behind her. They stood upright as soon as they reached the big cave. Siri found two more glow rods and lit them. They prowled around the cave, pawing through the bins in which Ona Nobis kept survival gear and protein packs.

"Can I help?" Astri asked. "What are we looking for?"

"Tools," Obi-Wan said. "Something to dig with."

Astri sighed. "Ona Nobis hauled out a bin of tools when she left. She didn't leave anything. Not food or water, either."

Siri sat back on her haunches. "We can't dig with our hands. We'll never get out."

A slight whimper from Tup ended in a howl as Cholly kicked him.

Siri's eyes roamed over the cave. Suddenly, she raised her glow rod. She rose to her feet in one quick motion and went over to study the wall of the cave.

"Obi-Wan, look."

Obi-Wan stood at Siri's shoulder. He saw that the cave walls were braced with slender metal poles.

"Do you think the cave would collapse if we cut a few of these down?" Siri asked.

Another moan from Tup. This time, Weez joined him.

Astri came closer. She gazed around the cave, noting the number of supports. "I'm no engineer, but I bet you can take some of these out."

"You'd *bet*?" Tup asked. "Aren't you sure?"

"I can't be sure," Astri said. "But if it's our only chance, it's worth the risk, isn't it?"

"No," Tup said in a small voice.

Astri turned to Siri. "What are you thinking of doing with them?"

"They're shiny," Siri said. "And they look pretty flexible. I'm thinking if we can get them through the rocks and sand, we can signal the outside."

Cholly looked dumbfounded. "What outside? It's just desert out there!"

"There's a tribe nearby," Astri said. "They scavenge for food. Someone might see it."

"Or someone could come looking for us," Obi-Wan said.

"Or the whole cave could collapse on our heads," Tup suggested. His hands fluttered down as he mimicked the cave ceiling falling on them. "Woosh."

"I guess we should take a vote," Obi-Wan said. He looked at Siri and Astri, who nodded immediately. Cholly followed with a nervous nod. Weez agreed with a shrug. Then he elbowed Tup.

"I guess it's better than starving to death," Tup said shakily.

Siri gritted her teeth. She activated her lightsaber and carefully began to slice through the slender metal pole. It peeled back from the wall and Obi-Wan stepped forward to grab it. A stream of dirt rained down on his head, and Tup fell to his knees and covered his head with his hands.

"Gibbertz and ham, we're done for!"

The stream of dirt stopped. Obi-Wan scrutinized the ceiling above. "It's all right," he said. "I think it will hold."

"He *thinks*," Tup repeated.

"Shut up, Tup!" Weez and Cholly yelled. Another stream of sand poured down.

"Come on, Obi-Wan," Siri said. "Let's see if we can push this through."

They wiggled through the opening and

crawled forward. It took trial and error, but first Obi-Wan, then Siri threaded the slender pole through crevices in the rocks. Siri hit a rock and wiggled the rod, trying to force it through. The rod snapped.

"We'll have to try another," Siri said.

This time, Tup rolled into a ball and kept his eyes closed as Obi-Wan sliced through the second pole. He eased it away from the wall and had to jump back as a chunk of loose dirt and rocks cascaded down. They heard a rumble overhead.

"Don't say a word, Tup," Astri snapped.

Siri and Obi-Wan went back to the cave entrance and tried again. He tried to guide the rod through the tiniest of cracks. He pushed, pulled, prodded, and maneuvered but he got no further. Sweat streaked through the dust on his face. His gaze locked with Siri's. An unspoken agreement passed between them. This time he closed his eyes as he gently moved the rod. Together they called on the Force. He felt it gather power around him. The sand and rocks were part of him. They were connected to everything around him. He could feel the tiny rivers of space through the packed debris.

Obi-Wan maneuvered the rod carefully. He felt it poke through. He wiggled it.

"I think it's out in the air now."

"Good. Push it out as far as you can," Siri breathed.

Slowly, Obi-Wan pushed the rod through until he only held the very end. He wiggled it.

"Maybe if the wind dies down, the sun will glint on it," Siri said.

Obi-Wan wasn't sure if the wind ever died down in that canyon, but he didn't tell Siri that.

For the next few hours they all took turns crawling through the narrow cave and holding the rod. They turned and twisted it carefully, in case it could catch a ray of sun.

The group split Obi-Wan and Siri's survival rations, but it did little to assuage their hunger and thirst. The air grew close and hot. They barely spoke or moved in order to conserve what little oxygen they had left.

When Obi-Wan's turn came again, he took the rod from a weary Tup. He lay flat and wiggled the metal. He was tired from the rescue of Qui-Gon and the battle with Ona Nobis. He could not remember the last time he had slept. But he would lie here and stay alert as long as he had to. As long as there was hope —

"Hello in there! Is anyone there?"

"Yes! We're trapped!" Obi-Wan shouted.

"I am Goq Cranna. Who is there?"

"Goq Cranna, it is Obi-Wan Kenobi! I am the

Jedi who visited your tribe and asked for your help!"

"Ah, then it is good I stopped. Stay back, young Kenobi. We will dig you out."

Obi-Wan crawled back into the cave. Siri, Astri, Cholly, Weez, and Tup sat propped against the cave wall, exhausted.

"Goq Cranna has found us!" Obi-Wan said. "He's digging us out."

"Thank the stars and planets," Tup said fervently.

It seemed to take a long time for Goq to dig out the opening. At last light streamed in and they saw the smiling face of Goq's son, Bhu.

They crawled out of the cave into the orange blaze of sunset.

"The wind dies down at dusk, or else we would not have seen the silver rod," Goq said. "Even though we were searching. We saw the dead pilot and knew Ona Nobis had been here. We went into hiding. But then when we emerged we met a pilot who was supposed to pick up two passengers at the landing platform. They didn't show up. Bhu said, what if the wonderful lady who saved our tribe is in danger? So I agreed to look. Bhu saved you."

Bhu smiled shyly at Astri, who hugged him. "Thank you, Bhu."

On their last trip, Astri had made a trade with

Bhu for information about Ona Nobis. She had taught the desert tribe how to find food in the harsh environment. It was obvious that Bhu now worshiped her.

Siri combed her hair behind her ears with her fingers, shaking out the sand. "Did you actually see Ona Nobis?"

"Close enough to touch," Goq told her. "I was nearby when she called someone on her com-link. Someone was trying to persuade her to do something and offered her a cut of a potential fortune if she did so."

"Did you hear if she accepted, or where she is headed?" Obi-Wan asked urgently.

"I merely heard stray words," Goq said. A look of blankness had come over his face. Obi-Wan recognized it. It was the look of a Sorrusian who did not want to get mixed up in a stranger's business. Obi-Wan shot a glance at Astri.

"Surely you picked up some indication of what she was up to," Astri said gently, her hand still on Bhu's shoulder.

Goq's eyes warmed as he looked at Astri and his son. Astri had saved his tribe. For that, he would overcome his Sorrusian instinct for self-preservation at all costs.

"I do know where she is headed, wonderful lady. Belasco."

*　　*　　*

Obi-Wan stood on the landing platform of Arra. The sunsets were long on Sorrus, and the sky was still ablaze with orange and yellow. He had just concluded a difficult conversation with Qui-Gon. It had not been easy to tell his Master that contrary to orders he had stopped in the desert before heading to Coruscant.

Now he waited out Qui-Gon's silence.

At last the Jedi spoke. "You were told to come straight to Coruscant."

"The stop, we felt, would have been quick. And I had a strong feeling that Astri was in danger."

"The stop was not quick, and you put yourself and Siri in danger as well."

"And now we know that Ona Nobis is headed to Belasco. It is the home planet of Senator Uta S'orn! She was Jenna Zan Arbor's only friend. This can't be a coincidence. Uta S'orn could be in great danger. We should go there immediately!"

Another long silence. "Adi and I are disappointed in both of you. We will discuss this later. For now, we will meet you on Belasco."

CHAPTER 12

Qui-Gon gazed through the cockpit of the consular ship that was ferrying the Jedi to Belasco. From high above, the capital city of Senta glowed. It had been built centuries before out of native rose-colored stone. It was a spectacular sight, crowning the golden hills that surrounded a sea of sparkling blue.

Casually, he stretched his arms and legs, testing his strength. His continuing weakness dismayed him. He knew he had not given his body a chance to recover. But he was driven on by his fierce desire to bring Jenna Zan Arbor to justice. He was the one who knew firsthand how her mind worked. He could not leave this mission to others.

"Do you feel you are regaining your strength?" Adi asked politely. He knew she would not ask such a personal question if she were not concerned.

"Yes," he said shortly. He liked and respected Adi, but he did not wish to tell her his concerns. He hoped that would be the end of the subject.

He should have known better. Adi was not one to pry. But when she wanted a true answer, she did not give up.

"I noticed that your connection to the Force was a bit weak back at the lab," Adi said. "I would not wish you to return to the Temple, or ask you to do so. But . . ." Adi turned her face to look at him directly. Qui-Gon was forced to meet her dark, commanding gaze. She was almost as intimidating as Mace Windu when she wanted to be.

"I just want things clear between us," she continued. "Here is what I see. You are pretending to have made a full recovery, but you have not. You compensate for your weakness by demonstrating your strength in strategy and decision-making. You should have consulted me before ordering Siri and Obi-Wan to Sorrus, Qui-Gon. I am your comrade. Not your enemy. If you have weakness, I should be aware of it."

Adi didn't let anything slide. Qui-Gon knew he had overstepped. He should have consulted his fellow Jedi Master before issuing the order.

"I'm sorry," he said. He did not find it hard to apologize when he knew he was wrong. That didn't mean he enjoyed it. "You are right on all counts. My connection to the Force has weakened along with my body."

"All right. Now I know." Adi turned to look out the cockpit windshield. "The landing platform is crowded. I don't see our Padawans."

"They had better be there," Qui-Gon said. He was still irritated that Obi-Wan had made the stop in the desert of Arra without consulting him. "Unless they decided to go off on their own mission again."

Adi gave one of her rare smiles. "They did well, and you know it."

Qui-Gon frowned. "They disobeyed."

"They had reason."

"They did not contact us."

"They are learning independence."

"At a cost of disobedience?"

Adi leaned back. "You know the Jedi look at things differently, Qui-Gon. We are not an army. Our discipline comes from within. Each Jedi has his or her own connection to the Force. We all are taught to trust our feelings and hone our instincts. Obi-Wan had a strong feeling and followed it. Siri backed him up. You did the same on Kegan, and I backed up your instinct — even though you did not ask my opinion. I am pleased that Siri is learning cooperation. Perhaps Obi-Wan has taught her more about it than I can."

"Obi-Wan is usually cautious," Qui-Gon said

as the ship began landing procedures. "Yet sometimes he is swept away by feeling. I worry about those times."

"As the Council worries about you," Adi said in an amused tone. "You and Obi-Wan seem so different. But at the core you are very alike."

"Perhaps that is not good," Qui-Gon mused. As the craft descended, he could just make out Obi-Wan standing, waiting for him.

Adi looked down at Siri, who was standing next to Obi-Wan. "It is the same for me. I see Siri's defiance and independence and see myself. In guiding her I guide myself. It is good that this is so."

Qui-Gon felt her words strike his heart. Obi-Wan's face was upturned now, his expression anxious. Being a Master was difficult for Qui-Gon. Pride in his Padawan battled with the need to be stern. He saw so much potential in Obi-Wan. He wanted to mold this being into a better Jedi than he was himself. He was impatient with himself as often as he was impatient with Obi-Wan. He saw that Adi was right: When he was stern with Obi-Wan, it was sometimes because he saw his own mistakes in the boy.

The consular ship slid into a narrow space among larger vessels. Adi turned to the pilot. "We do not know how long we will be on Belasco, but we might need to leave quickly."

"I will be on alert, waiting for your signal."

The landing ramp was activated, and Qui-Gon and Adi walked down to their Padawans.

Siri and Obi-Wan faced them, their gazes expectant. They awaited whatever their Masters might say.

Qui-Gon strode forward. "Next time, contact me first," he told Obi-Wan.

Adi spoke to Siri quietly so that the other Jedi could not hear. She preferred to give her Padawan instructions privately when she could. Then she turned back to Qui-Gon and Obi-Wan.

"I would say that our first step is to warn Uta S'orn that she could be in danger," she said. "I think we all agree that if Ona Nobis is here, Jenna Zan Arbor must have been the one who summoned her. And the fact that Zan Arbor picked her old friend's home planet can't be a coincidence. She must be planning to contact Uta S'orn."

"We have no proof to bring to Senator S'orn, only suspicion," Qui-Gon said. "But we owe her that, at least."

"We've learned that because of her years of service, she has been granted a home in the palace on the old royal grounds," Obi-Wan told them.

Qui-Gon nodded. "Then let us head there. But first, where is Astri?"

"She was nervous about seeing you," Obi-Wan said. "She feels badly that she put Siri and me in danger."

Qui-Gon glanced around. Amid the throngs of people standing on the landing platform, he glimpsed Astri standing next to the departure checkpoint area. A long line of Belascans snaked around her.

He walked closer. Astri looked thinner and more muscular, and her shaved head gave her a fierce appearance. She did not look like the soft, pretty girl he had known. But her eyes were the same, clear and honest. Right now they were filled with uneasiness.

"I'm so sorry," she said. "I did not think Obi-Wan would follow me. I would not ask for more help from the Jedi. You have done so much for me already —"

"All of which we were happy to do," Qui-Gon said. "And Obi-Wan's decision was his decision. But I am concerned, Astri. Didi is recovering quickly. He will find new investors for a new business. You must know this. Why are you still chasing Ona Nobis? I do not think it is because of the reward."

Her warm gaze grew hard. "She shot him as though he were nothing, just something in her way."

"Yes. She feels nothing for living beings. But

revenge makes one careless," Qui-Gon said. "Leave Ona Nobis to us."

She shook her head stubbornly. "I can't."

Annoyed, Qui-Gon fell silent. He could not control Astri's behavior. She was a distraction to the mission, but he could not allow her to go off alone. He was too close to her father and cared too much for her to watch her walk off into danger.

Qui-Gon sighed. "I have no right to tell you what to do."

"Now we agree," Astri said cheerfully.

"But I have a right to make a request," Qui-Gon added.

She looked at him warily.

"Remain with our party for the time being. Ona Nobis is here on Belasco. Either we will find her, or she will find us. You will learn more with us than without us."

Hesitantly, Astri nodded. "All right. I thank you."

"If you persist, I cannot protect you," Qui-Gon warned. "But at least I'd like you near."

Obi-Wan walked up. "Adi is feeling a disturbance in the Force."

Qui-Gon hid his dismay. He had not felt anything.

"All right," he said shortly. "Come, Astri."

"What about my friends?" Astri asked.

Obi-Wan glanced over. He saw Cholly, Weez, and Tup trying to make themselves inconspicuous nearby.

Qui-Gon frowned. "After years of disapproval of your father's friends, now you consort with criminals?"

One corner of Astri's mouth lifted. "They are not competent enough to be criminals. And I'm almost growing fond of them."

With a sigh, Qui-Gon beckoned to Cholly, Weez, and Tup. The trio came forward uneasily. "It appears that we are stuck with you," Obi-Wan told them.

"It is usually our policy to run away from trouble," Cholly said. "So don't worry."

The group headed over to Adi and Siri.

"Something is wrong, Qui-Gon," Adi told him in a low voice. "I'm feeling desperation and fear here. Look at the departure checkpoint."

Qui-Gon's keen gaze swept the Belascans in line. Now that Adi had alerted him, he felt what he should have known all along — a rippling disturbance in the Force. But he did not need the Force to alert him to the fear on the faces of the Belascans.

"You are right," he said. "And this landing platform is extraordinarily busy."

"Everyone seems to be leaving, not arriving," Siri observed.

"Let's walk a few blocks into the city," Adi suggested. "Maybe we'll pick up on what is wrong."

They took the turbolift down from the main landing platform to the city streets below.

"We did not have time to do much research on Belasco," Adi said. "Here is what we know. This is a wealthy world with a rigid class system. The planet was once ruled by a royal family, but now a Leader is elected, who then elects his own Council. Senators are greatly revered."

"And Uta S'orn is a favorite of the current Leader, Min K'atel," Obi-Wan said.

"Look," Qui-Gon pointed out. "There are clinics set up on almost every block. They look temporary. Maybe a sudden illness has infected the population. There aren't many people on the streets."

An elder Belascan sat nearby on his front stoop, his hands dangling between his knees, a lost look on his face. He wore the distinctive elaborate headwrapping of the Belascan people, but two loose ends of fabric trailed over his shoulders as though he'd lost interest halfway through the task. Adi walked closer.

"I'm sorry to disturb you," she said gently. "We have only just arrived on your world. We sense that something is very wrong here."

"Very wrong." The handsome elder turned a

bleak gaze on them. "Have you not heard? Our water supply is contaminated."

"We have not heard. You get your water supply from your Great Sea, do you not?" Adi asked.

He nodded. "It is run through the desalinization tanks and provides us all with drinking water. Every seven years, a naturally occurring bacteria invades. We prepare for this. We know how to contain it, and we stockpile water for our use while the scientists control the bacteria. This year, they could not control it. It has multiplied and spread. But not before it took the lives of many elders and children. Among them my granddaughter."

"I am so sorry," Adi said. She bent down slightly to give the man a brief touch on the arm. Underneath Adi's regal manner, her intuitive nature gave her insight into suffering.

"I am not alone," the Belascan continued. His bleak gaze swept the empty street. "Many are ill on Belasco. Even the Leader's own daughter. Most of the ill are children and elders. The Leader has set up med wards on the royal grounds. But every day there are more funerals. Even while all our scientists work to contain the bacteria, we are running out of water. And running out of time."

Adi bid the elder good-bye and turned to the

others. "This news is distressing. It can't be a coincidence."

"Jenna Zan Arbor must be behind this," Qui-Gon said grimly. "She has done this before, introduced a virus or bacteria into a population in order to rush in at the last moment and save it."

"We'd better get to the royal grounds," Adi said.

Hurrying now, they followed the curving streets to the palace, which was visible on the main hill of the city. The palace gates stood open to all so that the population could enjoy the gardens. As they walked through they could see that large temporary domes had been set up on the wide lawns surrounding the sprawling rosy palace. Medics walked rapidly by them, and some children sat on benches nearby. They wore white robes, and their thin faces were turned toward the sun.

Adi looked shaken. "If Zan Arbor is responsible, this is monstrous."

"Could she deliberately make all these children sick?" Siri asked.

"I'm afraid she could," Qui-Gon said.

Tup swallowed. "If she could do this to kids, imagine what she would have done to *us*."

They asked a medic for Uta S'orn's whereabouts, and he pointed them to a garden at the back of one of the Ward Domes. They found S'orn sitting on a bench, watching over a group of children. Instead of her usual jeweled head-wrapping, she wore one of fine white linen. A small girl with dark curls sat in her lap.

Uta S'orn was speaking to the girl with a smile on her face, but it faded when she saw the Jedi.

"This is a surprise," she said to Qui-Gon. She gave a disdainful glance to Astri, Cholly, Weez, and Tup. "Is this your new entourage?"

The little girl shrank shyly back against Uta S'orn's lap. Qui-Gon crouched down and smiled gently at her.

"And who are you?"

"Joli K'atel," she said, and added confidingly, "I'm sick."

"I am very sorry to hear that. But I'm sure you will be well again."

She nodded. "My father says it is so."

"Then it is so," Qui-Gon said gravely.

Uta S'orn gently eased the girl off her lap and gave her a gentle pat. "Go sit with the others, Joli. I need to speak to these people. Unfortunately."

The little girl wandered off, the sash of her robe trailing in the grass. Uta S'orn's face was creased with worry as she watched her.

"I have volunteered as a med aide," she said quietly. "I thought I could help. I did not know it would break my heart."

"Is that the Leader's daughter?" Adi asked.

"Yes. But she is no more important than all of these children," Uta S'orn said, waving her hand to take in the Ward Domes. "They are our future. We must save them." She turned to them. "What is it that you want? As you can see, I am busy. Why are you here? It seems I cannot get away from the Jedi."

"We have reason to believe that Jenna Zan Arbor —" Qui-Gon began.

She stood up angrily. "Not this again. You have told me what you believe about my former friend. I have not heard from her, nor do I wish to. She has nothing to do with me."

"But we think that she does," Adi said. "We think that she is here, on Belasco. We're not sure why. There could be some link that we are overlooking, some reason she needs to contact you again."

"But she hasn't," Uta S'orn said impatiently. "And I will not see her if she tries. All right?"

"She might insist," Qui-Gon said. "And she can. Ona Nobis is here as well. She has kidnapped and killed for Jenna Zan Arbor before."

"If you're trying to frighten me, it isn't working," Uta S'orn said dismissively. "I have no time to worry about phantom threats. My world is dying. I see now there was a reason I returned here."

"We are merely trying to protect you —"

"No need. I am safe here. Although we have no king, the royal droid guards still protect the Leader and everyone on the grounds. Thank you for your concern, but Ona Nobis cannot get to me here. Now if you'll excuse me, there are sick children to tend."

Uta S'orn walked away.

"I guess she has a point," Siri said, glancing around at the busy grounds as medics walked by and guard droids, their shells polished to a golden gleam, patrolled. "It would be hard for Ona Nobis to get to her here."

Qui-Gon and Obi-Wan exchanged a glance.

"I'm afraid, Siri, that in our experience," Qui-Gon said, "Ona Nobis can get anywhere."

CHAPTER 13

"Why didn't you tell Uta S'orn that we suspect Jenna Zan Arbor has engineered the bacteria explosion?" Obi-Wan asked Qui-Gon as they left the royal grounds.

"Because we have no proof, only our suspicions," Qui-Gon said. "She would not believe us. She doesn't even believe that Zan Arbor is here."

"Nevertheless, she will take care, just in case," Adi said. "Despite what she said, she is afraid of Ona Nobis."

"We have to get proof," Qui-Gon said.

"I'm confused," Siri admitted. "I don't understand why Zan Arbor would come to Belasco at all."

"We know that Zan Arbor killed Uta S'orn's son. Uta S'orn knows it, too. But Zan Arbor doesn't know that she knows — as far as she's concerned, Uta S'orn is still an old friend," Adi explained. "Perhaps Zan Arbor came here because S'orn is a powerful ally, and she needs her help."

"That could be," Qui-Gon said, nodding. "And Zan Arbor feels she still needs the protection of Ona Nobis as well. She knows we will be pursuing her. Yes, I think Zan Arbor will contact Uta S'orn. But we must convince S'orn that Zan Arbor is here. Let's go back to the landing platform. If we can prove that Zan Arbor landed on Belasco, Uta S'orn might listen. In the meantime, even if Zan Arbor used an alias, we should be able to track her."

"How can I help?" Astri asked.

"The royal grounds are open to all," Qui-Gon said. "And those guard droids seem to have a mostly ceremonial function. Someone needs to stay there and watch Uta S'orn. Ona Nobis could show up at anytime."

"We can do that," Astri said, with a glance at Cholly, Weez, and Tup.

"Do not approach her," Qui-Gon warned. "And remember — your best revenge is to bring Ona Nobis to justice. We can do this for you. Then you can collect your reward."

"That sounds like an excellent plan!" Tup beamed.

"I don't care about the reward," Astri said. "Only about her capture."

"Don't be so hasty," Cholly said.

Astri, Cholly, Weez, and Tup turned away from the group to start back toward the royal grounds.

"You're placing quite a bit of faith in them," Adi observed.

"Not really," Qui-Gon said. "I'm counting on Cholly, Weez, and Tup to be obvious. Ona Nobis might steer clear of Uta S'orn for a time if she knows they are watching. That will give us time to gather evidence that Zan Arbor is behind the poisoning of the water supply."

Obi-Wan's senses suddenly went on alert. Even while he was walking, he had been watching every shadow. After his last encounter with Ona Nobis, he was taking no chances. He had sensed a sudden movement nearby and realized that someone was following Astri.

He signaled Qui-Gon with a quick glance and melted away from the others. He ducked back into an alley and scanned the street behind. Whoever was following the group was moving quickly from one shadow to another.

Using his cable launcher, Obi-Wan swung himself up to the flat roof overhead. He ran lightly across the roof. When he reached the corner he stopped and waited for his target below to catch up. Then he leaped down, aiming to land directly in front.

To his surprise, he found himself face-to-face with Fligh. He was the thief back on Coruscant who had stolen Zan Arbor's datapad and given it to Astri, inadvertently plunging Astri and Didi into danger. Fligh was wearing an eyepatch and a stunned expression.

Obi-Wan was just as stunned as Fligh. Qui-Gon, Adi, and Siri ran up to them quickly.

"Fligh?" Obi-Wan said. "I thought you were dead. I saw your body on Coruscant."

"No, you didn't, Padawan," Qui-Gon said.

"But you did," Obi-Wan said, confused.

"No," Qui-Gon said. "I saw a body that resembled Fligh. I had my doubts."

"Ah," Fligh said. His face was naturally mournful, with a downturned mouth and sad eyes. "I've never been clever enough to fool a Jedi. Never will."

"What are you doing here now?" Qui-Gon asked.

"Following Astri, of course," Fligh answered. "I thought I owed Didi. Even though I keep losing her, I am doing my best, which isn't much. But there you go."

Siri sidled closer to Obi-Wan. "What's going on?" she whispered. "Who is this character?"

"Fligh is a friend of Didi's back on Coruscant," Obi-Wan explained quickly. "He's the one who stole the datapads of Jenna Zan Arbor and Uta

S'orn in the Senate building. Then he was murdered. Or so I thought."

"He looks pretty healthy to me," Siri observed.

"Hey, I lost my eye!" Fligh protested.

"I can see that. I'm sorry," Siri said.

"I mean my false eye," Fligh explained. "It was a beauty, wasn't it?" he asked Qui-Gon and Obi-Wan. "But I decided I had to leave it at the scene of my murder. It's those kinds of touches that convince people you're really dead."

"How did you do it?" Obi-Wan asked curiously.

"I have a friend who works at the morgue on Coruscant," Fligh explained. "And I think *my* job is tough."

"You don't have a job," Obi-Wan pointed out.

"Being a thief is a *job*," Fligh answered huffily. "I get up every morning and go to work, just like everybody else. But this particular morning, I realized that someone was trying to kill me. When you get a whip wrapped around your neck, it wakes you up to the possibility. Luckily my landlord is handy with an electrojabber. But I thought I should disappear for a while. So I spoke to my friend at the morgue, and he found someone with my general characteristics. Who was dead, I mean."

"We assumed that," Qui-Gon said.

"My friend did the rest. We drove the body to the alley and left it there. Along with my eye, alas. I knew the security police would not bother to run ID scans on the body — there are some advantages to being someone nobody cares about. Just another piece of riffraff meeting a sad end. They'd accept the text doc identification and just cart the body to the morgue. Nobody would shed a tear."

"Didi did," Qui-Gon said sternly.

Fligh brightened. "He did? He is such a good friend!"

"But why would Ona Nobis be after you?" Obi-Wan wondered aloud. "You didn't have Zan Arbor's datapad any longer. You gave it to Astri."

Fligh shrugged. "I was just a loose end, I guess."

"Oh, I think you were more than that," Qui-Gon said, crossing his arms. "You're leaving something out, Fligh. The body was found drained of blood. Why did you do that?"

"Because that was how Ona Nobis left her victims," Fligh responded. "Six of my fellow riffraff were found that way."

"But we didn't know that yet. No one had yet traced Zan Arbor to Ren S'orn, or any other victim. We didn't even know Zan Arbor had anything to do with the attack on Didi."

"Ah, Jedi logic, so impressive," Fligh said nervously. "Are you sure?"

Qui-Gon nodded. "Very sure. Which means that *you* knew Zan Arbor was behind the attack. And you knew she was conducting experiments that involved extracting blood from her victims."

"Hmm, interesting point," Fligh said. "I find I must agree. Maybe I *did* know that. Maybe I traced a few of the murdered riffraff to Zan Arbor's lab. Maybe that's why I stole her datapad in the first place. But I didn't see why it would help Didi to know that. At the time. I felt badly after he was hurt, of course. Maybe I should have warned him after all. Maybe I should be a better person in general. But at least I am watching over Astri while Didi is in your excellent Jedi hands. I'll protect her if anything happens. Of course," Fligh added quickly, edging away with an uneasy smile, "I am hopeless at protection and therefore delighted to see that the Jedi are by her side. Obviously, I am not needed, so I guess I'll just head off. . . ."

"Not so fast," Qui-Gon said, catching Fligh by the elbow. "I have more questions. What about Senator S'orn's datapad?"

"What about it?" Fligh asked.

"What happened to it?"

Obi-Wan looked at Fligh curiously. He hadn't

thought of the question, but he was interested in the answer. Once they had identified Jenna Zan Arbor as the one who had hired Ona Nobis, they had stopped investigating what was on Senator S'orn's datapad, or what had happened to it. It seemed a minor detail. But Uta S'orn kept connecting to the mission, whether she wanted to or not. Maybe there was a detail they had overlooked.

"I still have it," Fligh said. "I haven't had a chance to sell it yet." He slipped a small data-pad out of his tunic. "See?"

Qui-Gon took it from him.

"There you go," Fligh said, waving a hand. "I won't even ask for credits. See how generous I can be with stolen property? You will have to erase all those files on it. Just Senate holo-transcripts of speeches. Or leave them, and you can use them as a sleeping potion." Fligh made a loud snoring noise. "Take it from me. Very dull. Now, if you don't need me, I'll be going. This world is too depressing, even for me. I think I'll head back to the fun-filled world of Coruscant."

Waving, Fligh took off. Qui-Gon turned his attention to the datapad. He quickly accessed the files and searched through them. Obi-Wan watched over his shoulder. Hovercams recorded all Senate proceedings. Each Senator could download transcripts into their own datapads for official records. Senator S'orn had recordings of several speeches she had made.

Qui-Gon shut down the datapad. He glanced at Adi.

"What are you thinking?" he asked her quietly.

"I do not like how Uta S'orn keeps coming into this mission," Adi said. "Let's get to the landing platform."

CHAPTER 14

On the way to the platform, Qui-Gon contacted Tahl and asked her to investigate the odd bacteria formation on Belasco.

He was about to sign off when he had a thought. "Tahl, can you forward the official Senate hovercam transcripts from . . . hold on." Qui-Gon accessed the file listing and read out the dates and times.

"Sure," Tahl said dryly. "I just love dealing with the Senate bureaucracy. Nothing I like better."

"That's what I thought." Smiling, Qui-Gon cut the communication.

"Why did you ask Tahl to do that?" Siri asked.

"Just a hunch. I want to make sure the transcript on Senator S'orn's datapad matches the official filed version," Qui-Gon explained. "I've heard of senators bribing the operators to alter official transcripts for one reason or another. There must be a reason Senator S'orn has kept those transcripts on her datapad. Maybe we'll find out why."

At the docking platform, the Jedi headed for the official in charge of off-planet vessel registration. Transports to Belasco had slowed to a trickle as word had reached the galaxy of the water shortage. It was easy for the dockmaster to check the records over the past two days.

"That V-wing cruiser is unusual," the official said. "You don't see many of them in private use. I think I can find it . . . here it is. Registered to a Belascan native who was arriving home. Cir L'ani and one passenger."

"Do you have a record of the passenger?" Adi asked. "Can you give us a description?"

"Do you think I remember every ship that docks here?" the official asked, shaking his head. "Just the pilot of the vessel registered. That's all we require. Sorry."

They thanked the official and walked out onto the busy platform.

"It could be them," Adi said. "But we need proof."

"Let's ask a worker," Qui-Gon suggested. He gazed around the platform. "Why don't we each pick someone and see what we can find out."

The group split off. Obi-Wan stayed where he was. He scanned the different workers on the platform. Some were checking text docs, some directing transport, and some refueling ships. He did not know how to choose.

But then he noticed a young woman, dressed in the coveralls of a mechanic, who was working at the refueling bay. The young woman was busy doing her job, but as she worked she gazed at the different ships as they came in for landings. Something about the alertness on her face caught Obi-Wan's attention. This was someone who admired sleek airships. She would remember the V-wing cruiser.

He walked over and nodded a hello.

"If you need refueling, you have to signal the controller," the worker said. "Get a number and wait your turn. You can signal from your ship or go over there." She pointed to a booth a short distance away.

"I don't need refueling," Obi-Wan said. "I'm looking for someone. She landed in a V-wing cruiser. Black with silver underside —"

"I remember that ship," the young woman said, her eyes suddenly brightening. "She was a beauty. I'd love to get my hands on those controls."

"Do you remember the pilot and passengers?"

She wiped her hands on her coveralls, thinking. "I remember I was surprised. I expected some hotshot pilot to come strutting out of that cockpit. Instead there was a petite human woman and a sick old man. Her father, she said. I refueled them."

"How do you know he was sick?" Obi-Wan asked.

"Because he was taken out on a med-splint. I don't think he was conscious. A medic met them when they landed. A tall Belascan male."

That could have been Ona Nobis in disguise.

"Do you know where they went?" Obi-Wan asked.

The worker shifted her feet. She was constantly moving as Obi-Wan asked her questions. And she seemed so nervous. "No, but they had to file a flight plan." Gazing at Obi-Wan, she wiggled her foot.

Obi-Wan noticed the movement and looked down. A small hand was curled around the worker's ankle.

"That's my boy, Ned," she said in a whisper. "Please don't report me. I had to bring him to work this week. My mother is ill and she's the one who takes care of him."

Obi-Wan smiled down at the boy, who looked up at him. A small toy was clutched in his dirty fist. "I won't tell. Thank you for your help."

He hurried over to Qui-Gon to tell him what he'd learned.

"That sounds like a good lead," Qui-Gon said. "I'm sure the flight plan is false, however."

But Adi was more skeptical. "I would like better confirmation," she said. "There are many ill elders on Belasco. I'm not sure if this will convince Uta S'orn."

"I hate the thought of Noor being unconscious," Siri said worriedly.

"She drugged him, most likely," Qui-Gon said.

"If that was really Noor," Adi said.

Obi-Wan caught Qui-Gon's irritation. Adi's instincts were renowned, but she did not abandon her need for absolute facts. They needed proof. Suddenly, Obi-Wan remembered something that had nagged at him.

"Wait," he told the others. Then he hurried back over to the worker.

She looked at him anxiously. "I'll lose my job if you tell my supervisor about Ned —"

"Don't worry," Obi-Wan assured her. He crouched down and spoke to the boy. "That's a nice toy. Can I hold it for just a second?"

The friendly boy nodded and handed it to Obi-Wan.

It was a model of a tiny V-wing cruiser. It had been cleverly fashioned from slender threads tightly wrapped over bits of metal.

Obi-Wan fingered the threads. They had come from a Jedi's robe. Noor had only pretended to be unconscious. He had left them a clue.

CHAPTER 15

Now that they knew for sure that Noor was on Belasco, they had to discover why Jenna Zan Arbor had traveled there. Adi and Qui-Gon set up two datapads on board the consular ship. They ran the Senate transcript on one datapad, and Uta S'orn's on the other. Obi-Wan and Siri sat, watching intently.

"Look for the smallest difference," Qui-Gon advised. "There will be much talk, so listen carefully."

The holocam had recorded a session in the Senate that dealt with regulations in the Mindemir system. Senators got up and spoke endlessly about complicated rules. They interrupted one another and heaped praise and scorn on one another. They spoke for long minutes and said nothing.

Siri caught Obi-Wan's eye and faked a huge yawn. Adi saw the gesture.

"Every task requires full attention," she told Siri sternly. Then she turned back to Qui-Gon and murmured, "But I'm having trouble myself."

"I don't understand," Obi-Wan said. "Uta S'orn isn't even visible in the transmission."

"Exactly," Qui-Gon said.

Obi-Wan was mystified. He returned his attention to both transmissions, but it was hard to know what he was looking for.

At last a list of regulations was passed. The holocam hovered above as Senators rose to the front of their boxes to vote. The regulations were passed by a majority. Then, the screen went black.

"Shall we play it again?" Adi asked.

"Do we have to?" Siri muttered.

"Wait," Qui-Gon said. He scanned backward as the vote was called. "I think I know what is different. Here." He pointed to the screen on the left, which was the official Senate transmission.

"Look at the delegate from Hino-111," he said. He pressed the zoom function on the transmission for a closer view. "He is not pressing the 'yes' button. He is voting *against* the measure. Yet in the audio he is voting for it." Qui-Gon pressed the zoom function on the second datapad. "And here, he has recorded a 'no' vote. This is Uta S'orn's version."

Adi leaned closer. "She altered the official Senate record?"

"I'm sure if we study this we will find other votes that have been changed. The Senate recorder uses the official transcript to record votes. These regulations were never passed. Senators vote on thousands of regulations. Mindemir is a small system. It is a risky move, but this transcript is from eight months ago. Obviously, she got away with it."

"But why would she care about a regulation on Mindemir?" Obi-Wan asked.

"I'm sure she does not care for herself. She was paid to do this," Qui-Gon said. "Paid in credits or influence. The question is, who paid her?"

"Jenna Zan Arbor?" Siri guessed.

"That is what we need to know." Qui-Gon was already reaching for his comlink. "This is a job for Tahl." He walked away a few paces to speak quietly.

"Why would she keep the real transcript?" Siri asked. "It could incriminate her."

"For blackmail," Adi said. "She could always threaten to expose the person who engineered this. She could send it anonymously to the Senate. Perhaps she's covered her tracks so well that they could not tie the deception to her."

Qui-Gon returned with the news that Tahl would get back to them as quickly as possible. They reviewed the other transcripts. It was easier now that they knew what they were looking for. In each case, the votes had been altered.

By the time they finished, Tahl had signaled Qui-Gon.

"You are right," she said. "Jenna Zan Arbor conducted a series of experiments on the water supply of Mindemir. She needed a large planetary system to prove her theory, apparently. Endangering a whole system was of course against Senate regulations. But Senator S'orn introduced legislation that would allow this, if the planet's legislative body agreed to the experiment. The measure passed in the Galactic Senate and a few weeks later the government of Mindemir voted to allow the experiment."

"Easier to bribe a politician on a small planet to push through legislation," Adi said shrewdly. "But she needed someone powerful in the Galactic Senate."

"So we've linked Jenna Zan Arbor and Uta S'orn at last," Qui-Gon said quietly. "Zan Arbor said S'orn had been helpful to her. I did not think she meant S'orn had acted illegally."

"It is hard to believe," Adi said. "She has a reputation for great integrity."

"Eight months ago, Ren S'orn was still

alive," Obi-Wan said. "Jenna Zan Arbor was conducting her experiments on the Force as well. What if Senator S'orn knew this? What if Jenna Zan Arbor was blackmailing *her*?"

"So S'orn knew that Zan Arbor was holding her son, and she did what Zan Arbor asked?" Qui-Gon frowned thoughtfully. "It's possible."

"All the more reason to help Uta S'orn now," Adi said. "Whether she wants us to or not."

CHAPTER 16

Faced with the evidence, Uta S'orn crumbled.

"Yes," she said. "I altered the record."

She sat on a bench, her hands dangling between her knees. The grounds were quiet now, with most of the patients back in the Ward Domes.

"I had to," Uta S'orn said. "She had my son."

"So you altered the Senate record in order to save him," Adi prodded gently.

S'orn nodded. "And then she released him. But something went wrong. He was found dead. She told me that he had tried to break back into the lab, and Ona Nobis had killed him. I don't know whether to believe her, but what can I do? I broke Senate laws. My son is dead. The only thing left for me is to devote myself to the people of Belasco, the only way I can. I cannot imagine why Jenna would contact me again. She must be here for another purpose. Surely she will leave me alone now, after all she's done."

Usually, Uta S'orn's manner was brusque and impatient. Now Obi-Wan saw how deeply her grief ran. Her voice trembled, and her eyes were full of tears.

A tall man dressed in rich robes approached, followed by royal droid guards. Although his hair was silver, his face was youthful.

"Uta, are you all right? Do I need to eject these people?"

She hurriedly wiped her eyes. "No. This is our Leader, Min K'atel," she said to the others.

Qui-Gon and Adi bowed. "We are Jedi Knights Qui-Gon Jinn and Adi Gallia, and these are our Padawans, Obi-Wan Kenobi and Siri."

The Leader gave a short nod. "I don't care if you are Jedi, you are not to disturb Uta S'orn."

"They speak of things I'd rather forget," Uta S'orn said. "I don't mean to blame them, but —"

"Your distress is enough," Min K'atel said. He turned to the Jedi. "I must request that you leave the royal grounds. You have upset Belasco's greatest Senator."

"We are just leaving," Qui-Gon said politely.

The Jedi bowed and made their way out of the glade. As they struck out across the lawn,

Obi-Wan said, "I have never seen Uta S'orn so affected before."

"Yes, she seemed so," Qui-Gon said. "But you noticed she manipulated the Leader so that he would throw us out."

"She is lying," Adi said.

Qui-Gon shot Adi a quick glance. "You are certain?"

Adi nodded. "I don't know why. Something in her words is false." Her steps slowed, and she stopped. "I feel that he is here. Somewhere near."

"Noor is on the royal grounds?" Qui-Gon asked. "Let's return to Min K'atel and demand that he search."

Adi shook her head. "It's only a feeling."

"That is all we have! What good are your instincts, Adi, if you do not trust them?"

Adi met his gaze sternly. "I trust them. But I do not expect them to sway others. We cannot involve a government in our investigation without proof. You know that as well as I do."

Qui-Gon struggled with his impatience. His mind was tired, his body spent. He was not connecting to the Force as Adi was. His ragged nerves screamed for an end to this.

Adi had spoken to him of cooperation and loyalty. He would have to submit to her wishes now. She had just as much right to choose a direction as he did.

"What, then?" he asked. "What do you suggest?"

"Let us follow our suspicions to the logical next step," Adi said. "We must have permission to search those grounds. Min K'atel is not likely to give it to us as things stand. We will have to convince him. There is one last place to go."

Qui-Gon nodded. "The water purification plant. But we'll never get permission to enter."

"Then we'll just have to break in," Adi said grimly. "Yes, sometimes I do act on my instincts, Qui-Gon. The answer lies there."

CHAPTER 17

The plant was gated and heavily guarded. No doubt the security had been increased because of the bacterial invasion. The Jedi hovered in a heavily forested area on the fenced perimeter. Qui-Gon swept the area with macrobinoculars.

"There are none of the usual ways to breach security," he noted. "Anyone entering must go through a retinal scan. There are guard droids posted at every entrance. Even after we took care of the guards, we would have to break in with our lightsabers. And that would most likely trigger a full-scale security alert."

"We want to get in and out without being seen," Adi said.

"Not to mention without any loss of life," Qui-Gon added. He stared at the plant, thinking. Then, suddenly, he saw a way. "Of course," he said. "We can't walk in. But we can swim."

*   *   *

The Great Sea narrowed to a fast-moving river downstream from the plant. The water foamed around boulders and formed mini-falls in the center of the river.

"The current is very strong." Adi glanced at Qui-Gon. He saw the concern on her face. "Maybe it would be better if only one team goes in."

"We have a better chance if we all do." Qui-Gon took out his breathing tube and was the first to wade into the shockingly cold water.

"When we get to the indraw pipes, there will most likely be a filter covering the opening," Qui-Gon said. "We can't use our lightsabers, so we'll have to use vibrocutters. Stay close to us, Padawans. Do not be afraid to ask for our help if you tire."

And you, Qui-Gon? Will you ask for help if you need it?

Adi's dark gaze asked the question. He ignored it.

The Jedi slipped underwater. Qui-Gon felt the current pull him along. It was carrying him in the right direction, but he had to take care not to bump against the boulders or get caught in the swirling eddys. It took all of his strength.

The current swept them toward the pipes.

As they got closer, they felt themselves being sucked along even faster. Now the danger would lie in being slammed up against the filters.

As they approached the pipes, Adi motioned to them to fight the current. Waving their arms to slow their pace, they managed to gently bump against the giant filter. Already Qui-Gon had reached for his vibrocutter. He and Adi went to work as their Padawans hung on to the grates.

Quickly, they sliced a hole in the filters and motioned their Padawans through first. Immediately after entering the pipe, they were sucked along by the action of the water, bumping on the sides of the pipe, turning and tumbling until Qui-Gon did not know which way was up. His shoulder wound cried out at the twisting motion. By the time he spilled out into a giant tank, he was overcome with dizziness.

He felt Obi-Wan touch his shoulder. His Padawan had noticed his distress. Qui-Gon nodded to let Obi-Wan know he was all right even as he fought his queasiness.

They quickly swam to the side of the tank and swung themselves up and over the side. They were in a large viaduct made of stone. Banks of equipment surrounded the tank. Further on the water was treated, but here, machines took random samplings of its quality.

Adi pointed to a tech console nearby. While Adi, Obi-Wan, and Siri kept watch, Qui-Gon pressed buttons and levers until a long panel slid open. A storage unit held vials of water samples, labeled by date.

"We'll never get out the same way," Qui-Gon said to Adi as he tucked the samples into his tunic. "We'll have to find some tech jackets and pose as workers."

She nodded. "There's got to be a supply closet."

Suddenly, a red light on the console pulsed. A few seconds later, they heard the sound of approaching droids. "I think it's time to leave," Qui-Gon said, reaching for his lightsaber. "Let's do this quickly, before the Belascan guards arrive."

The guard droids wheeled around the corner, blasters held high. The Jedi charged as one spinning block, lightsabers in constant motion. Qui-Gon took out two droids with one stroke. Adi flipped over the group and attacked from behind. Siri went down on one knee and came up with a mighty swing that knocked one droid over and cut the other in two. Obi-Wan went for the droids on Qui-Gon's left side, slicing the top off of one droid and burying his lightsaber in the control panel of the other.

In just seconds, it was over.

"Belascan guards will be here soon," Qui-Gon said, breathing heavily. "Never mind getting out quietly. Let's just get out."

Together, he and Adi cut a hole in the dura-steel exit door with their lightsabers. A siren began to clang. With the noise ringing in their ears, the Jedi leaped through the hole in the door and raced for the high fence.

Qui-Gon reached out for the Force. He needed it desperately if he were to make it over that fence. He heard blaster fire ping near his ear. Obi-Wan and Siri sailed over the fence, clearing it by several centimeters. He saw that Adi had slowed her pace to make sure that he would be able to clear it.

With a mighty effort, Qui-Gon forced his tired muscles to cooperate. His feeling of the Force surged, helping his leap. Still, he slammed against the top of the fence and had to haul himself over by hand. Out of the corner of his eye, he saw Adi sail over.

Qui-Gon landed heavily and a little off balance. He raced for the treeline. He ignored the blaster fire behind him, counting on Adi to expertly divert any fire that came too close.

He reached the safety of the trees and glanced back. "They are not following. They don't have to. They know who we are."

Adi tucked her lightsaber back into her belt. "It won't take long before Min K'atel orders us off the planet. I think we just wore out our welcome."

CHAPTER 18

Qui-Gon leaned against the trunk of a tree, his eyes closed, as Adi ran the samples through an analyzer and then sent the data to Tahl.

Obi-Wan approached him and sat down gingerly. He knew that Qui-Gon did not want him to speak. But he was worried.

"You have not regained your strength, Master," he said quietly. "Are you sure that —" He stopped. Qui-Gon had opened one eye. That was enough to stop his voice in his throat.

"Winna Di Uni told me it would take time," Qui-Gon said. "It is doing so." He closed his eyes. "Do not worry, Padawan. This will be over soon. Then I will rest."

Obi-Wan nodded, even though Qui-Gon did not see him. He had observed his Master tired and in pain before, but never so diminished. It was a strange feeling. If Qui-Gon could weaken, any Jedi was vulnerable.

Adi's comlink signaled, and she quickly pressed the holo function. Tahl appeared.

"The bacteria have been bioengineered," she said without any preliminaries. "It has been cleverly done. The measures taken to restrain it actually caused it to grow."

Qui-Gon sat up, alert. "Can you tell the scientists here how to control it?"

"They already know," Tahl said. "A scientific research company on Belasco announced a discovery just a few hours ago. They now know how to neutralize the bacteria. They also have found a way to treat those who are already sick. They will make a fortune."

"A fortune," Obi-Wan repeated softly. "And a piece of a fortune was offered to Ona Nobis if she came back."

Adi leaned toward Tahl. "Can you trace the company back to —"

"Zan Arbor Industries? I already have," Tahl said.

Siri slapped a hand on her leg. "We've got her."

"Now we have to find her," Adi said.

"I'll be standing by," Tahl said, and her image faded.

Qui-Gon stood. "Let's head back to the royal grounds. I'm certain the answer is there."

The sun was lowering as the Jedi hurried through back streets toward the palace gates.

Streams of Belascan citizens were heading there as well. They realized quickly that news had spread about the discovery. The people were gathering to celebrate. They would have plenty of cover.

And so would Ona Nobis.

They moved through the crowd on the palace lawns, searching for Astri.

"I don't see her anywhere," Qui-Gon said. "She's supposed to be keeping an eye on Uta S'orn."

"There she is," Obi-Wan said, pointing. "She's wearing a medic aide coverall."

Dressed in white, Astri wheeled a young boy through the garden. She bent down to pull a blanket over his lap.

"It's good cover," Qui-Gon said. "But what about Cholly, Weez, and Tup?"

Tup burst out of one of the Med Wards at the head of a group of children, juggling three bright laserballs. Weez followed.

"At least they are staying out of trouble," Qui-Gon said.

Astri caught sight of them and hurried over, her face alight.

"Have you heard the news? A cure has been found!"

"We've heard," Adi said. "But we still have a problem."

"I've been keeping track of Uta S'orn," Astri said. "I haven't seen anything suspicious. She's out in the open all the time. She's devoting herself to the children. She does everything, even helps with food service."

Qui-Gon tensed. "Do you have access to the palace kitchens?" he asked Astri.

Astri nodded. "Food delivery is one place that they are shorthanded. Everyone can pitch in and help."

"Do you think it's possible to track the meals that leave the kitchens? Can you count the meal trays?"

"Yes," Astri said. "Cholly has been helping to prepare the trays."

"How are the meals delivered?" Adi asked.

"Through the tunnels, mostly," Astri said. "They were built about a century ago, during a war with a neighboring planet. It's the fastest way to get from the kitchens to the ward areas. They built the domes over the old entrances in the gardens, just for that reason."

"When is the next meal?" Qui-Gon asked.

Astri checked her timepiece. "Cholly should be preparing the trays right now."

"Good," Qui-Gon said. "Obi-Wan, Siri, I want you to go with Astri to the kitchens. Compare the number of food trays with the number of sick children. If there are more trays than children, follow Uta S'orn. Make sure she does not see you! Note where she delivers the trays. If Ona Nobis and Zan Arbor are on the grounds, they have to eat."

Qui-Gon fixed Obi-Wan and Siri with his most serious glare. "If you see, or even sense, that Ona Nobis is near, do not engage with her. Come back for Adi and myself."

Obi-Wan and Siri agreed and followed Astri to the palace kitchen. It was an enormous room filled with food stations and storage. Obi-Wan and Siri waited in the dim hallway while Astri went inside.

Cholly was busy setting up trays with bowls of stew, bread, and a fruit tart. Other workers milled about, dishing up the stew and pushing the trays forward in a line to be loaded onto carts.

Swiftly, Astri ran her eyes down the rows of trays, counting. She slipped outside to the hall.

"There are sixty-four trays," she said. "Two extra. Qui-Gon was right. Now we have to wait for Uta S'orn."

Moments later, the other workers began to fill the kitchen. They each took a cart and slid trays inside the warming element. Uta S'orn arrived and quickly worked to fill her own cart.

"I'll take Ward Five, as usual," she said.

She rolled the cart out into the hallway and

headed for the tunnel. Obi-Wan and Siri pressed back against the wall. They moved silently behind Uta S'orn, keeping as close as they dared through the twisting maze.

Uta S'orn delivered the meals to Ward Five first. They watched as she ascended the ramp into the ward. When she returned, she still had two trays on her cart. She made a sudden turn and came straight toward them.

Obi-Wan and Siri threw themselves back into a side tunnel. They flattened themselves against a wall and tried not to breathe. If Uta S'orn came down this way, they would be discovered.

They were lucky. She turned down an opposite tunnel. After a moment, they followed cautiously. The tunnel narrowed as it turned sharply to the left. Obi-Wan had been careful to keep track of how they were moving. He knew that they had turned away from the main wing of the palace and the wards and were heading toward Uta S'orn's private quarters.

Suddenly, they heard the cart stop. Obi-Wan crept forward. He peered around the corner long enough to see Uta S'orn place the trays on the floor. Then she turned toward him.

He ducked back and motioned to Siri. The two ran lightly down the tunnel, hearing S'orn behind them. She could not move as fast due to the cart. They reached the main tunnel and Obi-Wan headed left, guessing she was on her way back to the palace kitchens.

After a few moments Uta S'orn emerged and took the route Obi-Wan had predicted. Obi-Wan and Siri headed back the way they had come. They waited at the curve of the tunnel.

"What if Ona Nobis comes from behind us?" Siri whispered.

"We run," Obi-Wan whispered back.

To Obi-Wan's surprise, a small vent in the ceiling over the food trays opened. Ona Nobis slithered through, her Sorrusian skeletal system compressing to allow her to fit through the tiny space.

Siri's hand went to her lightsaber. She began to draw it out. In a swift move, Obi-Wan put his hand on her wrist to stop her. She glared at him, but he did not let go.

Ona Nobis picked up the sweet fruit tart from one tray and popped it in her mouth. Quickly, she gobbled up the second tart, then wiped her fingers delicately on her tunic.

"Sneak," Siri whispered in Obi-Wan's ear.

Ona Nobis pushed the food trays through the vent overhead. Then she hoisted herself up and through.

"We should have attacked," Siri whispered fiercely after Nobis disappeared.

"Siri, Qui-Gon told us not to," Obi-Wan said irritably.

"But we were so close! And she didn't have her whip," Siri argued. Her blue eyes glinted a challenge in the darkness of the tunnel, and she thrust her chin at Obi-Wan. "Or were you afraid to meet her again?"

CHAPTER 19

Adi and Qui-Gon listened to Siri and Obi-Wan's story. Adi gave a satisfied nod.

"They're here. That means that Noor is here as well." Adi glanced at Qui-Gon. "We have enough to speak to the Leader. We must take the risk."

"I agree," Qui-Gon said. "If we are lucky, we will avoid a battle. Whether Uta S'orn is being forced to hide Zan Arbor or not, he must be told."

Around them, preparations for a celebration had begun. The Leader had decided to throw a grand party for the city of Senta. More and more of the population streamed into the royal grounds. The gardens glowed with candles and lights. Musicians were beginning to set up near the flower garden. Servants, officials, and townspeople milled about on the lawns, fragrant with evening dew.

Min K'atel sat, beaming, with his wife. Their daughter sat between them, wrapped in a warm quilt. Uta S'orn sat to their right. As the Jedi walked toward him, Min K'atel's wide smile faded and he fixed them with a stony glance.

"I have received a report that saboteurs broke into the water purification center, no doubt to reintroduce more deadly bacteria," he said. "My security chief tells me these saboteurs were Jedi. Either you are impersonating Jedi, or everything I know of your order is wrong. Which is it?"

The Leader gave a signal, and the gleaming guard droids appeared, flanking the group of Jedi.

"We are neither saboteurs nor impersonators," Adi said in her strong, commanding voice. "We are Jedi Knights, come to find one of our own and to investigate your troubles."

"We do not need your help," Min K'atel said haughtily.

"But you need to know what we discovered," Qui-Gon said. "The bacteria in your water supply was deliberately introduced."

"You are strangers here," Min K'atel replied stonily. "You do not know that on Belasco, this bacteria arrives every seven years."

"We do know this," Qui-Gon said. "As did the person who bioengineered the bacteria to reproduce. She knew that you would not suspect that it was artificially introduced into your system because it was something you had seen before. But this bacteria was different. It was meant to multiply in response to the attempt to contain it."

Min K'atel stared at them. "And who would do this thing, and why?"

"Someone who stood to profit by eliminating it," Adi replied. "A brilliant scientist named Jenna Zan Arbor. She is behind the scientific group who will cure it, and she will make a fortune, enough to help her escape justice and remain a fugitive."

"She is not Belascan," Min K'atel guessed. "How could she do such a thing without help?"

"She had the help of a prominent Belascan who had access to areas of the highest security," Adi responded. She fixed her commanding gaze on Uta S'orn.

S'orn did not bluster or deny the charge. She raised an eyebrow and looked disdainfully at the Jedi.

Min K'atel glanced at S'orn. "This is preposterous," he said. "You try to cover your own involvement by accusing one of Belasco's finest citizens! I will contact the Jedi Council. I will not let this accusation stand!"

"Uta S'orn is hiding Jenna Zan Arbor and the

Jedi Master she is holding hostage," Qui-Gon stated. "If you would give the order to search her quarters, you would find them."

"I will not give such an order!"

Adi and Qui-Gon activated their lightsabers in a split second. Obi-Wan and Siri quickly followed.

"I'm afraid we must insist," Qui-Gon said. "A Jedi is being held captive on your grounds. That makes you responsible. If we must fight a battle to release him, know that we will."

Min K'atel looked uncertain. "There is no other Jedi here. Only wards full of sick children and elders."

"I saw a sick elder," Min K'atel's daughter, Joli, suddenly piped up. She shook the doll in her lap, moving its arms and legs. "He made this."

"And how did he give it to you?" Adi asked gently.

"He threw it down into the bushes," Joli said. "He threw down other toys to the children. Mine is the best." She smiled down at the doll in her lap. "It is the prettiest."

"Mine is the prettiest!" a young girl said, running forward, waving a doll.

"No, mine!" A boy shook a toy in the air.

Qui-Gon walked forward. He gently took the doll from Joli's hand. He held it against his robe. The color and texture of the threads matched exactly.

"Do you still say a Jedi is not on your property?" he asked Min K'atel.

Min K'atel's eyes traveled high above to the window where his daughter had seen the toy-maker. It was in Uta S'orn's quarters.

He did not look at Uta S'orn. "Search her quarters," he said to the captain of the guard.

Uta S'orn shrugged as the members of the royal guard rushed off. "They will find nothing."

"If that is so, then I will apologize most humbly," Min K'atel said. He turned to the guard droids. "Surround Senator S'orn."

The guard droids wheeled in formation. But instead of turning on Uta S'orn, they turned on the Jedi.

CHAPTER 20

"They have been reprogrammed," Qui-Gon said tersely.

The words had barely left his mouth when the droids began to fire. Blaster fire erupted in a flash around the Jedi.

Only the group immediately around them realized what was happening. The partygoers on the lawn thought the flash was part of the celebrations. They applauded as the Jedi began to spin, their lightsabers a blur. Musicians played nearby, and the people turned toward the music.

Obi-Wan thought of the many children surrounding them. His primary objective was to contain the battle so that they would not be injured by stray blaster fire. He knew the others had the same thought.

The droids stayed in formation, wheeling to attack and then regrouping. Uta S'orn slipped off her seat of honor and disappeared into the crowd.

The Jedi did not need to confer on strategy. Along with protecting the Belascans in the garden, they had to get to Uta S'orn's quarters. They formed a tight circle to deflect the blaster fire and attack the royal droids. As they fought, they moved steadily forward, fanning out to break the strict formation of the guards.

"Cover me," Qui-Gon said tersely.

Adi, Siri, and Obi-Wan stepped up the attack. They were a blur of movement now, moving together, covering one another and then reversing to deliver a furious attack on the droids.

Obi-Wan reached out to Adi and Siri, catching the rhythm of their battle strategy. Adi relied on Siri's quick footwork and gymnastic leaps. Siri depended on Adi's dazzling lightsaber action. Together, they were an amazing pair.

But even as they littered the grounds with broken droids, more arrived in what seemed to be a never-ending stream. They poured out of the palace guard room, blaster rifles pointed at the Jedi.

Fighting battle droids had its own challenges. Their weakness was the same as their strength: They did not think. They responded to stimulus. They saw beings as targets to be destroyed. Their complicated wiring could be compromised by one good blow. Yet their accuracy was impeccable.

Even as he fought, Obi-Wan kept in mind that Qui-Gon had run into the palace alone. He would meet Ona Nobis there. He remembered with alarm how Qui-Gon had not been able to clear the fence earlier. Qui-Gon needed backup.

He knew Adi was thinking the same thing. Without a word or a glance, they accelerated their drive with a furious series of volleys. They pushed forward until they were at the entrance to the palace.

Obi-Wan launched a quick reversal, sweeping up with his lightsaber, then leaping and twisting in midair to come down behind the droids. He attacked from behind, leveling four with two blows. Meanwhile, Adi and Siri slipped inside the palace. Obi-Wan leaped again, this time landing on the threshold of the entrance. With a backward kick that sent a droid flying, he raced inside.

The palace was dim after the blazing lights of the festival outside. Obi-Wan sensed rather than saw movement. Adi and Siri were heading up a grand staircase.

"This way," Adi called to him as she ran.

Obi-Wan started for the stairs. Suddenly, blaster fire erupted near him. Chips of stone flew from the step where his foot had been. He turned to attack, but his balance was slightly off. He knew his countermove would be clumsy.

He saw a blur near his shoulder. Siri had leaped from the top stair. She twisted in midair, holding her lightsaber high. As she came down, she sliced off the head of a royal guard droid.

"Thanks," Obi-Wan said.

"Anytime."

Obi-Wan raced up the grand staircase, Siri now behind him. He called on the Force to direct him, following the stir of air and heat that Adi had left in her pursuit. He ran down long corridors. Ahead, he heard the sound of shouting.

He burst into a high-ceilinged room. Jenna Zan Arbor stood in the center, her hands in front of her. Noor was bound and shackled with energy cuffs at his ankles and wrists.

"I am holding the formula for the eradication of the waterborne bacteria," Jenna Zan Arbor said, holding up a palm-sized datapad. "There is one crucial linkage missing from the version the scientists hold. Only I can cure this world. If you kill me, many will die."

Qui-Gon's lightsaber was held at his side. Adi stood near him. Obi-Wan had stopped short. He waited for the two Jedi Masters to decide on a strategy.

"We do not want to kill you," Qui-Gon said.

"Capture is death to me," Jenna Zan Arbor said. "It's freedom or nothing."

Adi and Qui-Gon did not look at each other. Yet Obi-Wan sensed that they were communicating. Noor's eyes were closed, but Obi-Wan felt the Force from him, as well. And this time Zan Arbor had no instruments to measure it.

He felt, rather than saw, Qui-Gon gather his strength. Obi-Wan felt its power.

Elation surged through him. Qui-Gon was back.

The datapad flew from Jenna Zan Arbor's hand and into Qui-Gon's suddenly extended left palm. At the same time, he leaped forward, his lightsaber slicing the air. Jenna Zan Arbor flinched, but he merely slashed at a hanging behind her. A large tapestry on the wall flipped over to land on top of her. At the same time, Adi sprang forward to free Noor.

Qui-Gon calmly tucked the datapad in his utility belt. He bent to capture Jenna Zan Arbor as she came up from underneath the tapestry, coughing from the dust.

"After all your experiments with the Force, in the end you failed to understand its power," Qui-Gon said.

She fixed him with a look of rage. "I should have killed you when I could."

"That," Qui-Gon said, "was your other mistake."

Obi-Wan looked around for Siri. She should have been right behind him. She was not. Alarm ticked inside him. Siri was always where the battle was.

And where was Ona Nobis?

Obi-Wan turned and ran back down the long corridor. He reached out to the Force, searching for Siri. She was close. He could feel her. In times of danger, their connection grew closer.

She was above him.

He raced to the staircase. It curved up and around and he lost sight of the top in the dimness. Obi-Wan dashed up the curving staircase. He paused at each landing but heard and felt nothing. She was still above him. At last he reached the top. A long corridor with thick carpets stretched before him. Frustrated, Obi-Wan paused. Siri was not on this floor.

He spied a small door to his right. Obi-Wan flung it open. He saw a narrow staircase twisting upward to the roof. In that instant he knew that Siri was up there and needed him.

He charged up the stairs, activating his lightsaber as he ran. He burst out onto the roof.

For a moment, his eyes were dazzled. The festival lights blazed far below. The lawns beyond were inky black. This portion of the roof was flat, but gables and turrets surrounded him.

He saw the pale violet glow of Siri's lightsaber. Her back was to the roof wall. Ona Nobis had her cornered. The laser whip wrapped around Siri's lightsaber, nearly wrenching it from her grasp. Siri placed her other hand on the hilt and held on, but she stumbled. Ona Nobis withdrew the blaster from the holster strapped to her thigh.

Obi-Wan charged, even as he reached out a hand to direct the Force. He could not count on his ability to move objects. But the Force surged this time, knocking the blaster from Ona Nobis's hand and sending her staggering slightly from surprise.

Obi-Wan did not stop, but leaped and twisted in order to come at Nobis from her other side, leaving Siri free to regroup.

The whip furled and his lightsaber hit it with a sizzle. Smoke curled upward. He twisted the lightsaber to release it. Ona Nobis reached for her second blaster.

Siri gripped her lightsaber and advanced. Sweat soaked her hair and tunic. Grimly she swung at Ona Nobis but the bounty hunter twisted away.

"Come on, children," Ona Nobis spoke at last. She bared her teeth. "You can do better."

Obi-Wan catapulted forward. He worked in tandem with Siri now, the two of them flanking the bounty hunter. This time when she furled her whip he leaped high to meet it, corkscrewing his lightsaber around and around so that the whip would tangle momentarily. He knew that Siri would take the opportunity to attack.

Blaster fire pinged next to him. It was very close. He hung in the air, holding on to the whip, every muscle straining.

She tried to twist the whip out of his grasp. Her strength was extraordinary. He felt his wrist wrench and he began to fall. The whip spiraled out, free again. He used his fall to twist one more time and surprise her with a roundhouse kick. Her second blaster flew from her hand and she let out a howl of rage.

Siri bounded forward to join him as he landed. Now they had her cornered. She restored the whip to normal mode and sent it flying high to wrap around a drainpipe nearby.

He saw that she meant to escape. She never stayed if she felt she was losing. She pulled herself up and over Obi-Wan and Siri, using the whip to propel herself high above their heads. For a moment her body hung motionless in the dark night sky.

She was holding on with one hand. What was she doing with the other?

"Siri, watch out!" Obi-Wan cried, as a third blaster appeared in Ona Nobis's hand.

At that moment, Adi charged through the door to the roof. She leaped high, slashing at the bounty hunter's whip. She neatly sliced it in two.

A surprised look came over Ona Nobis's tight features. She hung suspended in midair for one quick moment. Then, without the whip's support, she tumbled over backward and fell through the inky night far, far below.

CHAPTER 29

Qui-Gon, Obi-Wan, Siri, and Adi stood out-side the small building near the Senate on Coruscant.

"Ready?" Astri called.

"Ready," Qui-Gon answered.

Astri flipped a switch. Halo-lights glowed, spelling out

D I I'S N E W C A F

Astri sighed. "I guess it still needs work. That's what I get for using Fligh as an electri-cian."

"At least the food is good," Cholly said. He held up a chunk of spicy ahrisa. "This is the best I ever tasted."

"Mmmph," Tup agreed, his mouth full. Weez handed him a napkin.

Astri beckoned the Jedi inside and placed them at a center table. She poured tea for them.

"I don't like having Fligh as a partner, but he promised he would go straight," Astri said. "And he did find investors for us."

The cup stopped halfway to Qui-Gon's mouth. "Legitimate investors?"

"Of course!" Didi bustled forward from the bar. He had lost some weight during his illness, but had regained his rosy cheeks and merry temperament. "Fligh and I have learned our lesson."

"I hope so," Astri murmured. "All I know is, I'm keeping the financial records."

"I'm sure you'll be a great success," Adi said, toasting her.

Astri sat down at the table with them. "Have they set the punishment for Zan Arbor and S'orn?"

Qui-Gon nodded. "They have been exiled to a prison world for the rest of their lives."

"I can't believe Uta S'orn was an accomplice," Astri said, shaking her head. "Her best friend killed her son, and she still continued to do business with her!"

"Never underestimate the power of greed," Adi said soberly. "Uta S'orn wanted to make a fortune. Jenna Zan Arbor offered her that opportunity. She was the backing behind the scientific company on Belasco."

"Their plans nearly went awry when Zan Arbor was sidetracked by her interest in the Force," Qui-Gon added. "The fact that her friend had a Force-sensitive son was too tempting for Zan Arbor to resist. And when Uta S'orn found out what happened, her greed overcame her anger and grief."

"They are quite a pair," Siri said, grimacing.

Astri got up to fix the lunch she had promised to the Jedi. Siri beckoned to Obi-Wan and drew him into a quiet corner.

"I just wanted to say I was glad to see you turn up on the roof to help me fight Ona Nobis," she said. "I guess I thought less of you for fleeing the battle on Sorrus. I did not understand how powerful she was. She could have killed me, Obi-Wan."

"I cannot imagine that," Obi-Wan said. The embarrassment on Siri's face made him want to smooth over the situation. "You are the best Padawan fighter I've ever seen."

"Except for you," Siri said. "I have fought you in Temple exercises many times, Obi-Wan. I should not have questioned your ability or your nerve. I was wrong." The words seemed torn from her reluctantly.

"I have been wrong myself," Obi-Wan said lightly. "As well you know."

"Adi says I have learned an important lesson," Siri went on. She made a wry face. "And I hate learning lessons. I thought too much of my own abilities. Even though I'm a Jedi, I am not invincible. There are many in the galaxy who can defeat me. Now I understand why we were taught over and over that our motive must be sure, our concentration total. I underestimated the dark side of the Force. I will try not to do that again. And I know now that I will not always be strong. I will not be afraid to recognize when I am weak."

"An important lesson for Padawans," Adi said, overhearing them.

Obi-Wan threw a glance at Qui-Gon. "And for stubborn Jedi Masters."

Qui-Gon took a placid sip of tea. "I have no idea who you mean," he said, his eyes twinkling.